THE FEARLESS FIVE

Bannie McPartlin

Piccadilly
PRESS

First published in Great Britain in 2019 by
PICCADILLY PRESS
80–81 Wimpole St, London W1G 9RE
www.piccadillypress.co.uk

A CIP catalogue record for this book is available from the British Library.

ISBN: 978-1-84812-803-3
Also available as an ebook

2

Typeset by Palimpsest Book Production Ltd, Falkirk, Stirlingshire
Printed and bound by Clays Ltd, Elcograf S.p.A

MIX
Paper from
responsible sources
FSC® C018072

Piccadilly Press is an imprint of Bonnier Books UK
www.bonnierbooks.co.uk

To my chief advisor, Laura Kerins (aged 12),
your honesty (sometimes harsh) and insight
(always hilarious) were AWESOME.
Bannie loves you.

To all the kids who rock my world,
Bannie loves you.

THREE THINGS YOU SHOULD KNOW

Some people like to know more than others. I have a lot of story to tell, so to make sure that some of you don't get bored I'm going to add some extra things in the 'Three Things You Should Know' sections at the bottom of the page.

For example:
1. My cat would bite me to get at my chips.
2. He liked to chase cars.
3. He died under the wheel of a Ford Cortina with a mouth full of chips. RIP Mittens.

These are things you don't need to know but I think you should. It's your choice. You decide . . .

The Five

This is the photograph that hit the national news and made five kids the most wanted kids in Ireland.

From left to right: Sumo Lane, Walker Brown, Charlie Eastman, Johnny J and Jeremy Finn.

It's framed on my mam's wall over her prized white marble fireplace and next to my sister Rachel's nursing diploma and my brother Rich's gold record. The picture features my four friends and me, dressed head to toe in green, white and gold, our faces painted with shamrocks and harps and all of us grinning fiercely. We look nuts. We were nuts. We just didn't know it.

On the far left is Sumo Lane.

Sumo's real name is Brian, but he was never a Brian. Brians are mostly brainy and sometimes boring. He was neither of those. Sumo is huge. At twelve years old he's six foot tall and wider than a cottage door.

People moved out of the way when Sumo walked down the street. I came up with the name Sumo when we met, aged six, because even though he wasn't six foot then, he had jet-black hair, pudgy cheeks and he was always the biggest kid in the room. The name just stuck. Kids, teachers, parents (even his own) called Brian 'Sumo'.*

This is Sumo's best friend, Walker Brown. As you can see, he's skinny and tiny. He's thirteen in this photo, but he could pass for an eight-year-old.

---

* 1. I suspect Sumo's parents regretted picking the name Brian.
  2. Although he's a giant, he's gentle and kind.
  3. He's obsessed with comics and smells like Spam. Spam is disgusting sweaty pink meat that smells like feet.

We all wore Irish-flag-coloured, furry top hats, but Walker wore his reluctantly because he was serious about his hair. He kept the sides of his hair short and the top long. He backcombed it so that it sat like a giant slick wave on top of his head and it was so full of hairspray that it didn't move. A lot of effort went into Walker's hair, but it added almost two inches to his height so it was worth it. His big, thick, horn-rimmed glasses were so heavy he was always holding them against the bridge of his nose so that they didn't fall off. He had asthma, which meant he spent a lot of his time wheezing and sucking on an inhaler, so I used to joke that he was called Walker because he definitely wasn't a runner.* That always got a laugh. He's the only one not pretending to smile for the camera. He said we were crazy and that we'd get caught. He was right.

---

* 1. Walker isn't a nickname, that's his actual name. His mother just liked the sound of it, and because she is the bossiest woman in Ireland Walker's father gave in without much of a fight.

2. No one messes with Walker Brown. He's small but he's smart and mean as a snake.

3. Walker says the word 'fact' after any statement he considers important, and he thinks most of what he says is important. Fact.

Twelve-year-old Charlie Eastman stands in the middle and just in front of us. She looks like the leader of the gang here and (sometimes) she was, even though I didn't like it one bit!

The green Ireland shorts Charlie is wearing are so long on her they look more like baggy trousers, which wasn't something I noticed back then. Her skinny elbows point outwards as she rests her hands on her hips. That's what she did when she wanted anyone to know she meant business. She's winking under that big tall hat and that's her own red, wild and curly hair that goes halfway down her back. She painted her lips green to match the large shamrocks on each cheek. I didn't want her there that day. She was new to our gang and she'd bribed her way in, but the truth is, for what we were about to do (and it was seriously dangerous), we needed her.*

Beside Charlie, and with another mop of wild curls, is my very best friend in the world, Johnny J Tulsi. Thirteen-and-a-half-year-old Johnny J is the oldest of us. Everyone loves Johnny J, even adults. He's just cool.

* 1. Charlie is an expert tree climber and does deadly stunts on her pink Triumph 20 bike.
  2. She once walked home on a broken ankle! (After failing to stunt-jump over a dried-up riverbed on her yellow Triumph 20 bike, which broke in two!)
  3. She's crazy.

Johnny J didn't really look like the rest of us, who were pale-skinned, red-cheeked, pockmarked and freckled. He had smooth caramel skin, his father's brown eyes and mad curly hair, except his was light brown like his mother's.*

My mam always called him handsome and offered to feed him every time she saw him. Charlie followed him around like a shadow and giggled every time he spoke, even when he wasn't funny. (Charlie didn't find me funny at all, and I was officially the joker of the group.)

Johnny J always laughed at my jokes. We had the greatest conversations ever shared between two boys under the age of fourteen, and when I was scared or sad or nervous, he always knew what to say to make me feel better. We knew each other better than anyone else in the world and we told each other everything.

He's smiling in that photo even though his whole world was falling apart. I really admired him for

* 1. Johnny J s grandad had come over to Ireland from the Caribbean in the 1950s and married Johnny J's grandmother, who came from north Dublin.
  2. They had two sons. Both stayed brown even in winter, and everyone said that the Tulsis were the best-looking boys in the whole of Ireland.
  3. Johnny J's father married his mother, another Dublin woman (light brown hair and really pretty, with big blue eyes and a lovely smile), and they had Johnny J, who looked exotic, so all the girls loved him.

that. Johnny J was really brave. He was an only child and his father died in a car crash when he was only two years old, so when his mam got sick it was a real worry, but he never complained. Even when things got really bad and he knew his mam was dying. He never asked for help, but what kind of friends would we be if we didn't offer?

So this is me, Jeremy Finn, thirteen years and two weeks old, next to my best friend, with my thumbs high in the air and a big cheesy grin, pretending I had everything under control. (I didn't.) Spoiler alert: This does not end well.

And yes, I used to wear my brown hair to my shoulders (like a girl!), but I'd always worn it that way (I hated change and my mam thought it made me an individual).* Even with the wonky shamrocks my freckles are big enough to be seen. And you can't tell from the picture, but I'd had the runs for a week and I'd thrown up at least twice.

The headline in that newspaper clip screams 'Have You Seen the Fearless Five?' We had no idea what we were up against. We were foolish and we could have really messed our lives up, but we tried our best. That's what I think when I look at the faded old news clipping framed above my mam's prized white marble fireplace, next to my sister Rachel's nursing diploma and my brother Rich's gold record. *We tried . . . And we made a really big mess . . . And it was the saddest, scariest, weirdest, time in my life, but it was also the best fun I ever had.*

And it started here . . .

---

* 1. My headmistress makes me wear it in a ponytail and/or bun while on school grounds.

   2. Ponytails and/or buns are a brilliant way to carry pens and pencils around.

   3. I hated my freckles so much that my sixteen-year-old sister Rachel tried to get rid of them, when I was ten, by adding two spoons of bleach to one cup of lemon juice. She nearly melted my face off, but it did not get rid of my freckles.

1

The Match

It was 13 June 1990 and a game of football played in Italy between two foreign nations in the World Cup was a turning point for us, not just for my best friends and me but for the whole country of Ireland. We needed the Soviet Union to lose to Argentina. The Soviet Union's loss was Ireland's gain, and we advanced to the knockout stage of the World Cup and it was A VERY BIG DEAL. We were high on life, my friends and me. Anything seemed possible. I guess that's how the whole thing started.

So there we were, in the park, getting ready for a boxing match. We had just finished our very last day of primary school and we were looking forward to a whole summer of fun before heading off to our new secondary schools in September. Kids were everywhere and everyone was buzzing, still singing football chants and talking excitedly about football and how Ireland was IN THE WORLD CUP!

Johnny J was jumping up and down on the spot, his corkscrew curls bouncing in my face as I tried to glove him up. He was about to box against a boy called Fitzer. He was a right bruiser, bigger than Johnny J and a bully. He had a deep voice, greasy hair that just kind of dripped from his head and a faint dark moustache that stopped halfway across his top lip and just looked weird. Freaky Fitzer fancied himself as fast, strong and tough as nails.* Of all the lads who agreed to fight Johnny J, I figured he'd be the easiest to beat.

We charged one pound per kid to watch the fight, and one hundred and twenty-five kids turned up. Once we'd paid Fitzer the tenner we'd promised him and bought him a Mars bar (which we'd also promised him), our profit was one hundred and fourteen pounds and fifty-one pence, whether our

---

* 1. Freaky Fitzer was slow but mean.
  2. Freaky Fitzer was weak but vicious.
  3. Freaky Fitzer was about as tough as a bag of kittens, but he scratched like them too.

boy won or lost. It was a good thing too because Johnny J was no fighter. He just really needed the money for his mam.

Nobody named it back then, but we all knew that Mrs Tulsi had been battling cancer for a few years. It was obvious she wasn't getting any better. Johnny J was desperate. It was Walker who first mentioned that if she lived in America she'd be fine. The Americans were really medically advanced. At least that's what he said, and because he had won Young Scientist of the Year for his older sister April* and he was the only person we knew with a computer, we believed him.

'Mrs Tulsi needs to go to America. Fact,' he said. He convinced us that all we had to do was buy Mrs Tulsi a plane ticket and taxi fare and she could just walk into any hospital in America and they would welcome her in and fix her up in no time at all. Without the benefit of Google we believed him. We were naive, but if we didn't believe Walker, then what? Mrs Tulsi couldn't die! Johnny J left in this world with no parents at all?! Nah, I wasn't

---

* 1. He was too young to enter the Young Scientist of the Year, but he did all the work on her project.

2. She took all the glory.

3. He couldn't let it go.

13

having that. We were going to save her. We were going to save him. FACT!

I spent a lot of time worrying about Johnny J and his mam and his poor Uncle Ted, his dead father's brother. Uncle Ted was a really nice man who was always there for Johnny J and his mother. Every time he saw me he winked and told me I was a good kid, which was nice. No one else in my life did that. Uncle Ted was browner than Johnny J and had dark curly hair and wore cool clothes, like leather trousers and T-shirts with rock bands on them. He played the guitar and taught Johnny J to play when he was little. Johnny J said he could have been a rock star but he gave up music to take over running the family garage after Johnny J's father died. When Uncle Ted walked, he had a bounce to his step. I spent a lot of my early years trying to walk like Ted Tulsi, but it never happened. I just wasn't cool enough.

After Walker told us about America I'd lie awake in my bed thinking about all the things I could and couldn't do to raise money. Sometimes all that thinking made my stomach hurt. I was cursed with a nervous stomach. My mam said I took after my dad's mother, Nanna Finn, who spent so much time

14

in her toilet she had a bookshelf and plants and pruning shears in there. It was during one marathon cramp-fuelled thinking toilet session that I came up with the idea to start the boxing matches for money. Flights to America were really expensive back then, over a thousand pounds. That's a lot of fights for a boy who didn't really like to fight, but it was the only idea I had.

So there we were in the park. Freaky Fitzer and Johnny J danced and bounced around for a bit. Some of the crowd cheered. Some jeered.

'Go on, Johnny J. You can do it.'

'Smash his face in, Fitzer.'

'Get a move on, grannies.'

'Punch each other, muppets!'

The ring was just an area marked out by four coats, one in each corner. Sumo stood on guard, with his massive arms crossed and his legs spread wide apart and his chest sticking out. He looked like the bouncer who stood outside Barry's Betting Shop. It was Sumo's job to make sure the audience didn't push into the ring, and he took it seriously.

'All right, fellas, calm it down. Come on now. Give the fighters some space.'

Everyone shuffled back, and Sumo nodded to

himself and took out a Spam sandwich from his pocket, dusted it for fluff and demolished it in two bites. Walker sat at the picnic table, holding his big glasses against his face with one hand and counting out the money with the other. I stood in Johnny J's corner, hoping he wouldn't get killed, shouting words of encouragement while he bounced about on his tippy-toes. He bobbed and weaved and tired himself out before one punch was even thrown. I heard Charlie before I saw her. She was shouting down from somewhere in the sky.

'Keep your hands up. Come on, Johnny J, stop dancing, start hitting.'

It was *my* job to say encouraging stuff. *Annoying!* I looked up and there she was, sitting like Marvel Comic's Black Widow, spying on everyone with her flaming-red hair in two bunches either side of her head and her eyes flashing down at me from the highest tree. *Show-off!* Hollering away, *Oh look at me. I'm a girl and I can climb a tree!* Big deal. Not helpful at all. I was sick she was there because lately she was everywhere. Like a bad smell, she lingered and was hard to get rid of. I tried to nickname her Bad Smell but it didn't catch on the way Sumo or Freaky Fitzer had. *Disappointing.*

16

It was while Charlie was distracting Johnny J with her unhelpful comments that Freaky Fitzer let fly with his first punch. His right fist connected with Johnny J's left eye and it was game over as Johnny J hit the deck. Freaky Fitzer grabbed his tenner and Mars bar and was out of there before Sumo got Johnny J to his feet. The fight was over before it had begun.

2

The Knockout

In the aftermath of the quickest fight in history it became obvious from the loud booing and hissing sounds that the crowd felt they hadn't got value for money. I shouted to Sumo to escort Walker and the money away from the angry mob to a meeting point deeper in the wooded area of the park. Then placed myself between a dazed Johnny J and a bunch of mean schoolkids, trying to calm everyone down by assuring them that the next fight would be better.

'So who's fighting next?' someone shouted.

'Sumo,' I said, but I was lying. Sumo would never fight. He didn't believe in it. He said it hurt God or something. He could be a bit of a holy roller. (That's what my dad called people who went to Mass every day and judged people who didn't.)

There was a hush. 'Who'd fight Sumo?' a boy in the crowd said.

'Ah no,' another kid said. 'Sure he's got hands the size of frying pans!'

'Well, who's brave enough?' I said.

Every kid there looked the boy beside him up and down. No one spoke up. No one was brave enough.

'Tell your friends. The prize is twenty-five quid,' I shouted. There was a collective gasp. Twenty-five quid was a lot of money. They all moved off chattering among themselves and the terrible fight was forgotten.

Charlie climbed down from her tree. 'Nice one,' she said.

'Go away,' I said.

Charlie grabbed her bike. She was always on her pink Triumph 20. It was like it was attached to her. Johnny J was sitting on the grass, still slightly dazed.

'You OK?' she asked him.

'Yeah, grand.'

'I brought some frozen peas, in my basket. If you want to take some of the swelling down.'

'Ah yeah, cool. Thanks,' he said, and he placed the bag of peas on his eye. Johnny J was always polite to her, which really got under my skin. I helped him to his feet and we walked on. She cycled by his side.

'We're trying to do a little business here,' I said, hoping she'd go home.

'I know. I want to help.'

'Well, you can't.'

'I can fight,' she said.

Johnny J and I both laughed.

'Seriously. I beat up my brothers all the time. My dad said if I was a boy I'd be the next Barry McGuigan.'* Johnny J and I laughed again. Charlie Eastman really was the vainest person I'd ever met.

'You're not fighting,' Johnny J said.

'Don't know what you're laughing at. I'd win.'

'Against Sumo?' I said, and laughed.

'He'd just stand there, so of course I'd win, but I'd do some fancy moves to entertain the crowd,' she said, and she took her hands off the handlebars and started air-boxing as she cycled.

---

* 1. Barry McGuigan is the most famous Irish boxer of all time.

2. His nickname was the Clones Cyclone.

3. He had 35 professional fights and won by knockout 28 times. Charlie Eastman, the next Barry McGuigan . . . AS IF!

20

Johnny J laughed again, but this time it was with her not at her so I didn't join in.

'No girls fighting,' I said.

'Who says?'

'I say.'

'Johnny J?' she said, looking to him to stand up for her against me, as though that was even possible!

'He's right. Sorry,' he said.

'No one will pay to see girls fight,' I said. She stared at Johnny J, again waiting for him to back her up. He didn't.

'He's right. I'm sorry,' he said, and I wished he'd stop apologising.

She was hurt. 'Girls can fight. Girls can do anything,' she said, and it looked like she was about to cry. (Crying is another reason I really hated hanging with girls.)

We walked to the meeting place, where Sumo and Walker were waiting for us. Sumo rested his huge hands on Johnny J's shoulders. 'Show me,' he said. Johnny J took the peas away from his eye.

'Ohhhhhh, that's a shiner,' Walker said. Johnny J's eye was black, blue and even a little swollen.

'It doesn't hurt.'

'How much more do we need for the plane ticket?' I asked.

'A boatload more,' Walker said. 'We've only got one hundred and fourteen pounds and fifty-one pence.' A boatload was at least seven hundred quid.

Johnny J was worried. 'But we need to send my mam to America soon.'

'I know. We'll find a way,' I promised.

'The chemo is really hard on her,' he said.*

Johnny J looked so sad that it made Charlie well up. She didn't wail or anything. Tears just sparkled in her eyes, and when one escaped she wiped it with her sleeve and turned away.

I panicked. I couldn't deal with crying! 'Right! Fine! I'll fight. I'll fight them all.'

'It's no good, Jeremy. If Johnny J got knocked out first go, no one's going to pay to see you,' Walker said, before shrugging his shoulders and adding the word 'fact'.

'He's right. You'd be terrible,' Charlie said.

'Sorry, Jeremy – you promised them Sumo and

---

* 1. Chemo is short for chemotherapy. It's a treatment for cancer.
  2. Sometimes people lose their hair and get sick when they are going through treatment.
  3. It's really harsh and sickening, but back then before advances in science it was even worse.

22

you'd get pummelled,' Johnny J said, and coming from Mr Knocked-Out-In-One-Hit that hurt.

'I don't fight, and Jeremy can't fight,' Sumo said, folding his arms and widening his stance like that bouncer outside Barry's Betting Shop.

'All right, all right! What's this? National Pick-on-Jeremy Day?' I asked.

Sumo relaxed and put his arm around me in a kind of suffocating bear hug. 'But I think you'd be great,' he said, confusing everyone.

'You just told me I can't fight,' I said.

'I mean you'll be great at something else,' he said, and he smiled at me and patted me on the back.

'Cheers,' I said sarcastically.

He grinned at me. 'You're very welcome.' He was serious. He even gave me the thumbs up to prove he was serious.

Johnny J was quiet all the way home. We lived four doors down from one another. I used to pass my house to walk him home. Sometimes we'd sit on his front wall and talk for a while, but not that evening. When we got to his gate, we could hear his mam calling out for him through the open window on the second floor.

'I have to go.' He ran in and left the door swinging behind him. I stood there for a minute, long enough to watch him take the stairs two by two and disappear behind the bathroom door.

I shouldn't have stayed but I couldn't leave. I don't know why. I walked inside the small hall and I climbed halfway up the stairs, with the faded orange carpet that smelled of disinfectant and mint, and I sat listening to Mrs Tulsi throwing her guts up and Johnny J playing a game of I spy with her whenever she could talk.

'I spy, with my little eye, something beginning with *b*?' Johnny J said.

'Bruise,' Mrs Tulsi said. 'Do we need to talk about what happened?'

'I just fell.'

'No, you didn't,' she said, and then she threw up again. 'Should I be worried?'

'No, Mam. I swear. It's all good.'

'I spy, with my little eye, something beginning with *b*,' she said.

'Brush.'

'No.'

'Bath.'

'No.'

24

'I dunno. I give up,' he said.

'Bile,' she said, and he laughed.*

'Gross,' he said, and they laughed together.

'I can't do this any more, love,' she said, and Johnny J stopped laughing.

'Do what?'

'The chemo, love. I'm stopping it.'

'But it's keeping you alive!' my friend shouted in a voice that screamed panic.

'The doctors say it's time, Johnny J.'

'Ah no, please, Mam,' Johnny J cried out.

'It's not working any more, son. I'm so sorry,' Mrs Tulsi said, and although I couldn't see either of them, I could hear them crying. I instantly felt a combination of sadness and sickness, so I got up and ran down the stairs and out the front door and down the small pathway that led to the street and past the four doors that separated my house from Johnny J's, their terrible conversation echoing in my mind.

---

* 1. Bile is a dark green or yellowish brown fluid produced by the liver.
  2. Sometimes when you throw up violently bile comes out.
  3. It's gross and also a bit scary.

3

The Family

When I reached home, Dad was in the garden, leaning over the railings talking to the neighbour, Mr Lucey,* about Ireland qualifying for the World Cup.

'I tell you, the country will shut down for the next game. We'll never see anything like it again. Even the missus is coming to the pub,' my dad said.

'Sure the whole country's taking the day off,' Mr Lucey said. 'There won't be a man, woman or child in Ireland not watching that match.'

---

* 1. Mr Lucey smelled like cabbage.
2. He was sixty and lived with his ma.
3. He had a face liked a well-chewed toffee.

'I was over in Rolands' Garage earlier – they have to stay open, so they've only talked the granny into minding the shop for the match,' my dad said.

'Go on! Sure she's a hundred if she's a day.'

'Nah, she's in her seventies, but she spent a lot of time in Spain,' my dad said.

'Ah,' Mr Lucey said. 'God love her, she's got the face of a battered leather sofa.' (He should talk.)

'Sun's a killer, Lucey,' my dad said. 'And I wouldn't thank you for it.'

'I'd take a bit of sun to get over to see those lads play in Italy,' Mr Lucey said.

'Oh God, I'd sell one of me kids for tickets,' my dad said, before noticing I was sitting on the wall listening to him. 'There you are, son.' He didn't apologise for threatening to sell me. He just smiled and carried on talking. 'I tell you, Lucey, I'd die a happy man if I could travel to see those boys play for Ireland.'

'Do you know something? I think the real fun will be here. I'm telling you, Ron,'* he said, and he wiped his nose with the sleeve of his jumper,

---

* 1. My dad's name was Ronald, like the McDonald's clown, but people called him Ron.

2. His favourite food was a Big Mac.

3. He was terrified of clowns.

27

'the streets will be empty, every pub will be full and it will be something. Mark my words,' he said, and my dad nodded solemnly.

'You're not wrong, Lucey,' he said. They parted, and my dad went inside.

My dad and Mr Lucey were excited, jubilant even, and I felt terrible, because even though the best thing ever was happening to Ireland, the worst thing was happening to my best friend. I sat on my small front garden wall, battling the urge to throw up while thinking about Mrs Tulsi and wondering what lay ahead for Johnny J if she died.

I thought about going to Sumo's den to hide away for a while. He was an only child so he was treated like a king. The thing is, Sumo didn't want much. All he cared about was Spam sandwiches and collecting comics. He had the whole Marvel Universe comic collection. It was through Sumo I discovered Iron Man, Spider-Man, the X-Men, the Avengers, the Hulk, Captain America, Black Widow and the rest. We spent hours poring over his comics, arguing which superhero was stronger, faster, better or which villain was the most evil, most dangerous or scariest. Sumo liked his own space, which made sense seeing as he was a giant. His father was a builder, so to mark his eighth birthday he built him his very own den in the back garden. It was a large room, with a video recorder, an Atari games console and a ghetto-blaster stereo. He also had a TV, a sofa and two armchairs, so for a kid who didn't want much he had everything.

The first time I walked into that den (it quickly became our den), it was the absolute coolest moment of my life. I was home! After that we hung out there all the time, even when Sumo wasn't around. If life in the Finn household was getting too much for me, I'd go and watch a video or play a game of Space Invaders* on the Atari or read a comic in Sumo's den. It was always open. I was always welcome. It felt safe. It was our sanctuary.

Mrs Lane was very good about respecting that. She knocked when she brought in sandwiches, tea and biscuits. Sumo lived on Spam sandwiches. Mrs Lane always made enough for everyone, but that just meant that Sumo ate enough Spam sandwiches to feed a roomful of kids. He could clear a stacked

---

* 1. Space Invaders is a two-dimensional shooter game in which the player controls a laser cannon by moving it horizontally across the bottom of the screen and fires at descending aliens.
  2. By today's computer-game standards it's terrible.
  3. It's also pretty great.

plate of them in under two minutes. It was a sight to see. Even though Sumo had a super-cool den, an Atari, a telly, a video recorder and thousands of comics, he always said he'd swap it all for a little brother or sister. Did I mention before that Sumo was nuts?

I checked my watch, but it was too close to dinner to go anywhere. I exhaled loudly and with a heavy heart made my way inside.

I was the youngest in my family. My sister Rachel was nineteen and studying to be a nurse. She lived away from home and visited every now and again with her posh boyfriend Rupert, who was studying to be a doctor. He wore a wool scarf even in summer and spoke like he was gargling marbles. All my friends said my sister was beautiful, and when she walked by, boys stopped and stared. It was gross. She had blonde hair like my mam's, about my length, freaky blue steely eyes that shone in the dark and she had a bad temper. Rachel did not like her stuff being touched and she hated being told what to do, but if you didn't touch her stuff and stayed out of her way, most of the time she was pretty nice.

My brother Rich was fifteen, and while I was

tall, he was short. Looking down on my older brother was cool, except for the fact that it made him work harder to make my life difficult. Despite being small he was strong, and if he managed to get me in a headlock I was done for. He had short brown hair, small brown eyes, stubby little fingers and really sharp fang teeth either side of his mouth. My mam wanted him to get them filed down before he did himself damage, but Rich thought they made him look dangerous. He also liked singing and dancing and was in a boy band. When he wasn't putting me in headlocks, licking his sharp teeth, singing or dancing, he was bossing me around. He called me Numbnutbutt instead of Jeremy. He was hoping Numbnutbutt would catch on, but it was just too hard to say.

My mam was the real boss in the house. Dad didn't seem to mind, because while she was busy bossing, he could fade into the sitting room and settle into his favourite chair with his feet up, a newspaper on his lap and either news or sport on the telly. My dad was the local butcher, so he knew everybody. Everyone liked my dad because he took care of people during the bad times; when people had nothing and were struggling to feed themselves, they went to my dad. We weren't rich. We lived in a small house that hadn't been decorated in twenty years, but it smelled of roses and my mam always boasted you could eat your dinner off the floor it was so clean. Rich tested that theory when he tried to lick a dropped ice cream from it and she threatened to belt him with a wooden spoon.

My dad's hair went grey in his twenties and he grew a long beard around that time too. He never shaved it, and Mam said it made him look very handsome. We were mostly a happy family.* I still wished I were an only child like Sumo and Johnny J. Johnny J didn't mind being an only child. He had his mam and his Uncle Ted and that was enough for him. They didn't have a lot of money. Uncle Ted did his best to help out, but his garage had struggled too. He let all his workers go and fixed cars by himself. Johnny J helped out every Saturday. He brushed the floor and bought the sandwiches from the shop across the road. He cleaned the cars and he fetched the tools Uncle Ted needed when he was under a car. When he turned

---

* 1. My mother and sister killed each other over clothes.
  2. My brother lived to make my life hell.
  3. My father pretended not to notice when my mother and sister were screaming at one another and Rich was sitting on my head.

32

eleven, Uncle Ted taught him how to move a car from the service area in the garage into the car spaces outside. It was in a very small space and under his uncle's watchful eye, but he was driving and that was the coolest thing ever. When he wasn't working in his uncle's garage, hanging with us or minding his mam, Johnny J spent time in his room, playing guitar. He was lucky not to have anyone to burst in and deliberately mess up his bed. He had peace and privacy. He had a sign saying 'Do Not Enter' on his bedroom door and he swore that Mrs Tulsi didn't ever go in. My mam would have taken a bulldozer to my door if I dared to put a sign up. My sister Rachel got her temper from Mam. I used to wish I was Johnny J, before his mam got really sick.

4
The Idea

A week before the Freaky Fitzer fight fiasco we were sitting on the footpath watching other kids playing football on the green. I was a Man U supporter, Johnny J was a Liverpool man. We were arguing about who was the better team. Then out of nowhere he turned to me.

'I overheard Ma and Uncle Ted talking last night,' he said.

'And?'

'And . . .' He stopped talking for a moment or two. He put his hands in his corkscrew curls and shook his head like he was shaking them out. I knew it meant he needed a minute, so I just looked out at the kids playing football.

'Auntie Alison thinks I should live with her.'*

I got such a fright I jumped up. 'What?' I shouted. 'You can't,' I said. 'She lives in England!'

'I know,' he whispered.

'Ah no,' I said. 'No, no, no.' I really wasn't taking it well at all.

'It will be OK. I won't have to go. My mam won't let that happen,' he said, trying to comfort me.

'What did Uncle Ted say?' I almost screeched.

'Nothing. He just got real quiet.'

'Ah no,' I wailed. 'Well, you can't go!' I said. 'And that's it.' Then I started crying so much that green snot rolled from my nose to my chin and I coughed till I nearly choked. It was embarrassing and more than a little shocking.

Johnny J knew I didn't cope well with change.†

'Don't start wetting the bed again,' he said.

'We agreed we'd never talk about it,' I mumbled.

---

* 1. Auntie Alison was Johnny J's mam's sister.
  2. She was very successful.
  3. She thought we were all yokels. At least that's what my mam says, and I believe her. Note: Yokels are ignorant and unsophisticated.
† 1. Everyone said so – Mam, the GP, the principal of the primary school, the school nurse and that specialist fella Mam brought me to see after she and Dad went on holiday to Wales.
  2. They left us with Auntie Valerie for a week.
  3. I wet the bed for six months after that.

And all of a sudden he looked like he was going to cry, and he NEVER cried. 'I can't leave my mam, Jeremy. I don't want to live in England.'

'Well, that's good, because you're not going anywhere,' I said, and I really believed it. I COULD NOT LOSE MY BEST FRIEND!

He didn't bring it up again and neither did I. Instead we put our efforts into fundraising to send Mrs Tulsi to America. From then on I noticed him talking to Charlie more. I didn't know why and I didn't like it.

Charlie Eastman's mother was a district nurse. She visited sick people in their homes and helped them with their medication. She started visiting with Mrs Tulsi the year before. In the beginning Charlie would sit on the wall outside alone, waiting for her. Then one day Johnny J joined her. The next day was when she started following us around on her bike.

Charlie had three older brothers, Louis, Sean and Ben. Ben was still in school but the others were finished and working in the local paper factory. They all had red hair, and Louis, the oldest, had a mad red beard. I knew them because they were all huge fellas and brilliant at hurling.

Mrs Eastman was a redhead too, and so was Declan Eastman, her husband and the children's father. You could spot the orange hue of Eastmans from a mile away, and still Charlie had a way of creeping up on me that made me anxious.

Walker Brown spent a lot of time being anxious. He said it was because of the asthma attacks. He always had to have an inhaler on hand because if he didn't he could die. At least that's what he said. Mam said that breathing into a brown bag would work just as well, but then Mam believed that flat 7Up could cure every disease on earth, so she wasn't exactly reliable when it came to that sort of thing.

If Mam was bossy, Walker's mother was like a sergeant major. Sheila Brown walked around the place in tight trousers, high leather boots, shirts and blazers. She wore her hair in a tight bun, and when she gave you a certain look, it was hard not to poo in your pants. Her husband Denis drove a security van for the bank. Johnny J always joked that he must be really well paid or must've robbed a few quid every time he was in the van because Walker and his family lived in a fancy house and Denis Brown was the only one we knew who travelled to Italy for the matches. When I told my dad that Denis Brown was in Italy, he shook his head and said, 'I never thought I'd envy that man,' before he took himself to bed for a lie-down.

Walker had three sisters, April, May and June (I kid you not). They were triplets and they were eighteen and living in a flat in London. Walker had been what my mam described as a surprise. Rich said surprise was code for unwanted, before telling me I was also a surprise! I once asked Walker if he liked having three sisters. He said he hated it.

'Girls are evil,' he said. 'Fact.'

Walker really wished he was an only child too. 'Genius kids thrive without siblings. If it weren't for April, May and stupid June, I could be an astronaut by now.' He was ten when he said that and he really believed it.

Even though my brother made my life hell, and Sumo was sometimes lonely, and Walker's sisters held him back, we were all lucky. Every time we witnessed Johnny J holding his sick mother's hand, sitting in the back of an ambulance with the doors closing on them, we were reminded of how lucky we really were.

So not only was Johnny J's horrible Auntie Alison

threatening to steal him away to England, now his mam was giving up chemo! This was worse than bad. I sat on my front wall after Dad and Mr Lucey had gone inside, thinking, until the sky threatened rain and my mam threatened to murder me if I didn't get in for my dinner.

Over dinner Rich talked about his stupid boy band. Dad read the newspaper and my mam pretended to listen, but it was obvious her mind was somewhere else.

'Numbnutbutt, did you hear what I said?' Rich asked.

'I don't care what you said.'

'Yeah, well, I don't care that you don't care what I said. We're nearly ready to gig any day now.'

'No, you're not – you're terrible.'

'What would you know?' he said.

'I have ears.'

My dad laughed. Rich punched me in the arm.

'Ouch,' I shouted.

'How terrible?' Rich asked, poised to give me another dig, and then all of a sudden my mam started bawling. It was terrifying. She and Mrs Tulsi were friends. *She knew.*

Rich stopped talking. Dad stopped reading his

newspaper. He just placed his hand on hers and nobody spoke. She sobbed and mumbled, 'I'm sorry,' and sobbed some more. It must have only been seconds but it felt like hours.

'Why don't you boys eat your dinner in front of the telly tonight?' Dad said.

We were up and gone before he'd finished the sentence. We didn't speak, we just sat with our food on our laps listening to grown men talk about football. As soon as we were finished we disappeared into the safety of our own rooms.

I kept a walkie-talkie by my bedroom window. Johnny J had given me one of a set his uncle had bought him a year earlier. The reception was bad but we made it work. I picked it up, opened my window and sat on the window ledge and pressed the button.

'Number One Buddy, this is Brown Bear. Come in. Over.'

There was nothing.

'Number One Buddy, this is Brown Bear. Please come in. Over?'

Still nothing.

'Number One Buddy, this is Brown Bear. It's going to be OK. We'll fix it. Over.' Then I saw the window open and he leaned out and stared right at me.

'Promise? Over,' he said, and I nodded.

'Promise. Over,' I said.

I went to bed that night worried. Every conversation I'd had and heard that day spun around in my head. The kids in the park booing and hissing and the sound of everyone crying. I was terrified that Johnny J would have to move to England to live with his auntie and I couldn't stop thinking about my promise. *It's going to be OK. We'll fix it.* But how?

Then I remembered what Mr Lucey had said to my dad about the World Cup. He said the whole country would shut down for the Ireland games, but Rolands' Garage was staying open and the granny would be minding the shop for the match! And that was it. That was the moment I decided that if we were going to save Mrs Tulsi's life and I was going to keep my best friend living four doors down from me, we had to rob Rolands' Garage during the Ireland v Egypt match. Every other person in the country would be otherwise occupied. It was our big chance and I knew it was a mad idea, but it was the only one I had.

5

The Den

The day after the boxing match all the boys were in our den when I got there. And Charlie. It really bothered me. She had no business being there.

'What's she doing here?' I asked as rudely as I could. I didn't care. The den was ours. A girl-free zone. There used to be a sign up on the door that said 'No Girls Aloud', but it fell off in a storm and blew away. I really missed that sign.

'I invited her,' Johnny J said, and he gave me that stern look that said 'Back off', so I did. I didn't need the distraction anyway. I had a plan to deliver. Everyone sat down and I stood at the front of the room.

'So I've been thinking . . .' I started to say.

'Don't burst a blood vessel,' Walker said, and the others laughed, even Charlie. The neck of her, laughing at me in our 'Boys Only' den!

I flushed red, but I wasn't going to be discouraged so I pushed on. 'We need to rob Rolands' Garage.'

'Excuse me?' Walker said. He couldn't believe what he was hearing. To be fair, when I said it out loud it did sound mad.

'The Ireland–Egypt match is on the seventeenth. That's three days from now. Every man, woman and child in this country is going to be glued to the telly. That includes the coppers. I know for a fact that Jim Roland's granny is going to be looking after the garage that day so the Roland men can go down the pub . . .'

They were all dumbfounded. I knew they were dumbfounded because all their mouths were wide open. A piece of Spam fell from Sumo's.

'You want to rob a granny?' Walker said, pushing his glasses up his nose and looking around for someone else, anyone at all, to say something. No one spoke. I think they were in shock.

'I'm pretty sure she'll sleep through it,' I said with great confidence.

'Why?' Charlie asked.

'Because that's what grannies do,' I said.

'I mean, why are we robbing Rolands'?'

Johnny J cast his eyes to the floor. He couldn't look at anyone. Even me.

'Because we can't hang around any more. We need to get Johnny J's mam to America fast,' I said, and Sumo, Walker and Charlie stared at Johnny J.

He covered his ears with his hands and placed his face in his lap the way he used to do when we were kids and he didn't want to play any more.

'Oh!' Charlie said.

'Oh,' Walker said.

'OK,' Sumo said. 'We'll rob Rolands'.' He shrugged as he said it.

Walker looked outraged. 'What? Have you lost your minds?' he shouted at Sumo, but Sumo just shook his head from side to side.

'It's Johnny J's mam, Walker.'

'There has to be something else we can do,' Walker said.

'Good, great, I'm all for that, and when you come up with a better idea, let us know. In the

44

meantime, we're robbing Jim Roland's granny,' I shouted. I didn't mean to shout. It was all very stressful.

Walker stood up and started to pace the floor. Over and back, like a demented caged animal.

'What are you doing?' Charlie asked.

'I'm thinking,' he growled, then he coughed and spluttered and all of a sudden he couldn't catch his breath, so he pulled an inhaler out of his pocket and sucked on it hard.

'Sit down,' I said. He sat down and put his head between his legs.

Sumo raised his hand.

'Yes, Sumo.'

'You said Jim Roland's granny would probably be asleep. What if she's not asleep?' he asked.

'Good question, Sumo,' I said, and he nodded happily. 'Do you remember when my mam went to New York?' I asked.

'Do we what? You talked about it for six months. *Look at my cool American sweatshirt. Look at my cool American jeans*,' Walker said between deep breaths.

I ignored him. 'Well, she brought back some pepper spray. It's totally illegal, but she figured that Rachel might need it to protect herself from madmen when she went to nursing school.'

'Pepper spray? The stuff that blinds people?' Walker said, clearly alarmed.

'It only temporarily blinds people. It also causes difficulty breathing, a runny nose and coughing . . .' They were all staring at me like I was nuts. 'It only lasts about half an hour!' I said, trying to redeem myself.

'You want to use pepper spray on a granny?' Sumo said.

'No, of course not. We'll just threaten her with it.'

'Ah I don't know. That's not on. She could have a heart attack,' Sumo said.

'She'll be grand,' I said.

'She probably won't know what it is,' Charlie said, and I wasn't sure if she was being helpful or not, so I just scowled at her.

'Maybe I could just put her in a headlock?' Sumo offered. We all ignored him. That was a stupid idea.

Johnny J took his hands away from his ears and raised his head. 'How much do you think we'd get?'

'Enough to get your mam to America that's for sure,' I said, and he nodded thoughtfully.

'Are you sure you want to do this?' he asked, and I nodded. 'Then I'm in,' he said.

Walker's face fell and Sumo sighed deeply before tucking into a plate of Spam sandwiches his mam had made and left earlier.

'Me too,' Charlie said.

I shouted, 'NO WAY!'

'Yes way.'

'Nobody asked you! Tell her, Johnny J.' I mean honestly – a girl robbing Rolands' with us?! That was just ridiculous.

'I really appreciate it, Charlie, but Jeremy's right. You can't come,' said Johnny J.

'I can and I will,' she said, resting her hands on her hips to let us know she meant business.

'It's not happening,' Johnny J said.

I noticed the other two boys remained silent.

'Oh, it's happening,' Charlie said. 'And if I'm not with you, I'm against you.'

'What's that supposed to mean?' I said, and I'll admit I was screeching a little.

'I'll tell.'

'You would never!' I said, but I knew she would. Girls are such telltales.

'You need me for this to work, and if you don't

bring me I will tell, because getting in trouble with your parents is better than you getting caught by the police.' She was deadly serious and acting like she was doing us a favour. Charlie Eastman thought she was Clint Eastwood.* I was so enraged I had to fight with everything in me not to have a full-on meltdown.† I balled my fists up and really tried hard to control my temper just like my mam had told me. *Count to ten, Jeremy, and breathe.* One, two, three, four, five, six . . . I got to seven and realised everyone was staring at me like I was nuts.

'What makes you think it won't work without you?' I said through gritted teeth.

Charlie stood up and turned her back on me and faced the other three. 'Because my brother worked there for two summers. I know every inch of the place. Including where they keep the petty cash in the back.'

---

* 1. Clint Eastwood is a cool American actor who has played cowboy gunslingers, gangsters, heroes and dirty cops.

2. Charlie is a really annoying, wild-red-haired twelve-year-old girl.

3. Just because she wasn't afraid of anything did not make Charlie Eastman Clint Eastwood. *As if.*

† 1. When I was eleven, I went through a phase of having temper tantrums and total meltdowns at least once a week. I don't know why.

2. Once I kicked a hole in the wall. (How was I to know it was only plasterboard!) My dad threatened to have me arrested. I believed him.

3. I stopped having tantrums just before I turned twelve. My mam said I grew out of them. I think it's because I didn't want to go to jail.

Ah nuts!

'So does the granny know you?' Walker asked.

Good question. I wished I'd thought of it.

'I met her once or twice, but I'll wear my brother Louis's helmet to disguise myself. Jeremy can do the talking. I'll just nip into the back and grab the cash,' she said. She had it all worked out in seconds, like some kind of criminal genius. It was very disturbing.

'OK,' Johnny J said.

OK! OK?! What do you mean, OK?! I felt sick.

Charlie jumped up and roared. 'YES! I'm in!' Then she turned to the other two boys. 'And what about you two?'

Sumo was still shaking his head from side to side. He was rocking back and forth a little too.

'Yeah, of course, but no, it's wrong! But for Johnny J. Oh I dunno, it's not legal. It's not right,' he said.

'No, Sumo, robbing grannies and garages is not legal, but if it saves Mrs Tulsi it *is* right,' I said.

'I'm a Young Scientist winner,' Walker said as though someone had just asked him to list his achievements to date.

'So what anyway?' I said.

'It means I'm too smart to go to prison.'

'No one's going to prison,' I said.

'Robbers go to prison,' Walker said. 'Fact.'

'Only if they're caught,' Johnny J said, and Walker sighed, a heavy sigh.

'FINE! I'll do it, but only if Sumo will too.'

I could tell Sumo was worried about God crying. 'OK,' he said. 'But *I am not* pepper-spraying any grannies.'

'Fair enough,' I said. No one wanted that.

6
The Plan

Once we were all in agreement I revealed my plan. It was a simple one really. We dress up in the Irish colours, paint our faces green, white and gold and wear large, silly, furry, Irish-flag-coloured hats. That way we'd be partially disguised during the robbery and we'd blend in with the rest of Ireland after it.

'How do we get away?' Charlie asked.

'Our bikes,' I said.

'What if the money's too heavy?' Walker said.

'It's Rolands' Garage, not the Central Bank,' I said.

'So we'll take a small bag of money each,' Charlie said, and the others nodded.

'OK,' they said.

'OK,' I said. 'We're doing this.'

I pulled Johnny J aside. 'We're bringing the pepper spray, just in case any big burly grown men arrive,' I said. He nodded. 'I need your help getting it.'

Sumo had a blackboard on a stand. I pulled it into the centre of the room and started writing a to-do list.

TO-DO LIST

1. Break into Rachel's room and get pepper spray*/ NO PEPPER-SPRAYING GRANNIES. (Sumo insisted I write that.)
2. Beg, borrow or steal football costumes (including face paint).
3. Make sure bikes are oiled and chains are fixed.
4. Steal cash from Jim Roland's granny.

Now it was time to talk about the plan. I cleared my throat and stood in front of my friends (and Charlie).

'In three days' time the Ireland match is due to start at 4 p.m. in the Stadio La Favorita in Palermo.'

---

* 1. Rachel was private.

2. She had major trust issues.

3. She locked her bedroom even when she was away.

'My dad's going to be at that,' Walker said.

No one cared. I wrote the date and time on the board. I didn't write the venue or city as I had no idea how to spell them.

'The match will play for minimum ninety minutes, plus fifteen minutes half-time. That means we have between 4 p.m. and 5.45 p.m. to rob the garage.' *Easy. We only needed five minutes.* I wrote down '45 minutes to rob the garage' for all to see. Charlie nodded. The boys looked concerned. I reviewed the board.

THE PLAN

   3.30 p.m. Meet in the den and put on our football gear (including face paint).

   4.00 p.m. Grab the bags (stashed the night before) in the park.

   4.20 p.m. Cycle to Rolands' Garage.

   4.30 p.m. Rob Jim Roland's granny.

   4.35 p.m. Cycle to the forest and hide the money.

   4.45 p.m. Cycle to Cornally's pub.

   5.00 p.m. Blend into the crowd at Cornally's.

I thought it was an excellent plan, but the boys were still quiet, so I wrote:

JOB DONE. EASY. NO ONE HURT. JOHNNY J'S MAM SAVED.

I underlined 'Job done' and 'Johnny J's mam saved' for emphasis. Charlie nodded. The others still looked a little stunned.

'Any questions?' I asked.

'I've two questions,' Walker said.

'OK.'

'Can you hear yourself? And have you lost your mind??'

'Yes, I can, and no, I haven't. Any other questions?'

Johnny J had a question. 'What if something goes wrong?'

'Good question. If anything goes wrong, scatter. Cycle in different directions, ditch your bikes, run to the nearest pub and blend in with the crowd.' I was really pleased with that answer. I'd really thought it through.

Walker put up his hand.

'Yeah?' I said.

'I have asthma,' he said, and we all stared at him.

'Pubs are my enemy,' he explained, and we ignored him. He put his hand down and fixed his glasses on his face, mumbling to himself about dying in prison.

'What about the money? Where do we hide it?' Charlie said.

'In our place in the forest,' I said.

'Where's that?' she asked.

'I'll show you later,' Johnny J said. I didn't like her knowing our secret spot, but times were desperate.

'So we scatter, drop the money off at the hiding place and then blend in with the crowd,' she said.

'Exactly,' I said. *It's on the board, Miss Know-It-All.*

'OK,' Walker said, and he held on to his big glasses and shook his head. 'Madness . . .' he mumbled to himself.

Everyone took in the plan. They read and reread the board. I was scared and my stomach still hurt, but I felt proud. I had promised my best friend I'd come up with a solution to get his mam to America and I'd done that, and anyway, what could go wrong? *Nothing*. I genuinely believed that it was a perfect plan and everything would work out.*

That evening, at home, I sat with my dad and we watched a post-match analysis of Yugoslavia v Colombia. I wasn't really paying attention. I was thinking about my mam crying the night before. I wanted to tell her not to worry and that everything would be OK. But I couldn't trust her not to blow her top. I couldn't risk the operation.

That night before I went to bed I told her I loved her. I didn't really do it that often because, well, you know . . . it's embarrassing, but I did it anyway and I gave her a hug. I got a fright when it looked like she'd cry again, and felt a little uncomfortable when she didn't let go for a really long time, but when we pulled apart she was smiling.

'I love you too, son. You're such a good boy.'

I went to bed hoping that she'd feel the same way after I'd robbed Rolands' Garage.

---

* 1. It was a terrible plan.
2. Maybe even the worst plan in the history of plans.
3. I just didn't know it.

7
The Key

It was two days to the robbery and I woke up feeling scared and experiencing a constant flutter in my stomach, which put me off my food . . . But other than going hungry and having an unfortunate case of the runs, I really did feel good. *It's going to be fine.* The first thing on my list was breaking into Rachel's room for her pepper spray. I knew that the key had to be somewhere close so that if a fire did start in my sister's empty room, my mam could race in there to put it out with one of her three fire blankets or four fire foam sprays.*

---

* 1. My mother's main worries in life revolved around fire, famine, flood and nits. She lost her mind every time we got nits.

2. She also had a deep suspicion that all strangers (including grannies and kids) were potential muggers.

3. My dad used to say, 'Sometimes your mammy is mad.' He was right. He also said, 'Sometimes we're all mad.' He was right about that too.

So I just needed to work out where my mam would hide the key to my sister's room. She was out of the house and working a part-time job in the local supermarket, and Rich spent most of his free time rehearsing with his band in the garage. He'd told Mam he'd take care of me and then whispered in my ear that if I came anywhere near him or the shed he'd skin me alive.

When Johnny J arrived, Rich and the band were caterwauling in the garage, giving us space and time to find the key. We checked everywhere – kitchen, sitting room, hall table. We searched high and low but we just couldn't find it. Upstairs we tore through drawers (even my mam's underwear drawer!).

'Is this really necessary?' Johnny J asked while standing behind me as I (painfully) sorted through my mam's knickers.

'She keeps all kinds of things in here,' I said, pulling out her passport, a dog lead (we didn't have a dog) and a spare TV remote control. 'People put keys in drawers, don't they?'

'No, I mean the pepper spray,' he said.

'No one – not even an old lady – is just going to hand the cash over because we ask nicely,' I said.

Johnny J slumped to his knees. 'I dunno,' he said.

I joined him on the floor. 'What don't you know?'

'Robbing a place, it's serious.'

'So is losing your mam,' I said, and he looked so sad my stomach turned upside down and for a second or two I thought I might vomit. When the feeling passed, I stood up and put my hand out. 'Sorry,' I mumbled. 'I shouldn't have said that.'

He looked up at me. 'You're really sure the Americans can fix her?' he asked.

'The Americans have been to the moon, Johnny J. They can do anything,' I said, and he smiled. He reached for my hand and I hauled him up.

'Yeah. That's true. OK,' he said. 'Let's do this.'

When we'd searched everywhere we could think of in Mam's room, that only left Rich's room.

'Why would it be here?' Johnny J said, holding his nose as he entered. It smelled of cheap aftershave, old socks and hair gel.

'Well, it's not anywhere else,' I said.

'Who does your sister think she is anyway?' Johnny J said.

'The Queen of Sheba, according to my dad.'*

'I mean what is so important that she needs to lock it away?'

'Her stuff,' I said. Rachel's stuff was really important to Rachel. She hated anyone touching it. She lost her mind anytime Rich or I went near her room.

Johnny J and I riffled through my brother's room. We found a box of fireworks, including Roman candles, French bombs and whistlers. We also found a packet of damp cigarettes and a bow and arrow! My mam would have hit the roof if she knew – ever since Cyclops Brennan lost his good eye in a slingshot accident, my mam decreed that anything that involved flying weapons through the air was not a suitable plaything and therefore contraband. If I wasn't planning an armed robbery of Rolands' Garage I could have blackmailed my brother for a long time.

We could hear the band from the shed. Rich, aka Spots, Buzz, Fingers and Cap had formed their band 'Fingers & the Fudge' six months earlier.

---

* 1. The Queen of Sheba was queen of a place called Sheba.
2. She thought she was it.
3. So did my sister.

None of them played an instrument. Fingers was the lead singer, and the lads all backed him up. Cap sang a lot too, but Fingers was the star of the show. They just sang to karaoke backing tracks, and although Fingers and Cap could both sing in tune, their voices didn't really work together, and Rich and Buzz were rubbish.

'They're hard to listen to,' Johnny J said, nodding toward the window.

'Tell me about it,' I said. I was having nightmares. 'I think Rich wants you to join them. He keeps talking about how good you were in the school hall,' I said. 'You wouldn't, would you?'

'I'd rather put my noodle in a blender,' he said.

After that we must have blocked them out because neither of us noticed when they stopped singing.

'Where does your mam put the spare house key?' Johnny J asked.

'In a plant pot beside the door.'

'Right,' he said. 'That's what my mam does. It's always close by and obvious,' he said, and he walked to Rachel's door. He looked on the floor. There was no plant pot. He looked at the door

61

and he reached up and sitting on the ledge was the key! He held it before my eyes and smiled.

'Nice one,' I said, and punched him in the arm. It was my way of saying 'Good job'.

I was halfway under Rachel's bed when I heard Rich come thundering up the stairs.

'Numbnutbutt? Hey, Numbnutbutt, you up here?'

Ah nuts!

8
The Band

Johnny J closed Rachel's door quietly and quickly and put his finger to his mouth.

'Numbnutbutt! Come out, come out, wherever you are,' Rich sang out. My heart started to race. If he found us in Rachel's bedroom, we were done for.

We could hear him walking in and out of the bedrooms.

'You better not have left this house without telling me.'

Johnny J and I stayed silent. Neither of us moved and we held our breaths.

'Where are you?' he called out, and he banged on the wall.

Johnny J pointed under the bed. He got down on his belly and he crawled under. I followed. It was really dusty under there and I was sure there were spiders. I wanted to sneeze, but I held my nose. I tried to forget I was lying on the floor in a tight and dusty space. My stomach was doing somersaults. Johnny J spotted the box of pepper spray. He pointed vigorously and mouthed, 'IT'S THE PEPPER SPRAY!' I nodded furiously and gave him the thumbs up. He grabbed the box and we waited.

'NUMB . . . NUT . . . BUTT!' Rich screamed one last time, and I could tell he was directly outside Rachel's door. Johnny J and I stared at one another, me holding my nose and him holding on to the box. We were under Rachel's bed for a minute, but it felt like an hour. Eventually we heard him running down the stairs and the back door closed with a slam. We both scrambled out from under the bed and I sighed a sigh of great relief. Johnny J held out the box of pepper spray so I could open it and take one of the two cans out. I handed it to him.

'This is it,' I said. There was a cobweb hanging from his ear. It was gross. I pointed to it. 'Spider house,' I said. I don't know why – the fright might have made me forget the word 'web'. He brushed it off and examined the can intently as we walked onto the landing. I locked Rachel's door and put the key back up on the ledge.

'Do we even know if it still works?' he said.

'What do you mean?'

'Well, does it have an expiry date?'

'Ah no, I don't know,' I said. It had been under Rachel's bed for two years.

We looked at the tin, but it said nothing about expiration. It was just covered in red Xs and health warnings.

'We should test it,' I said.

'On who?' Johnny J said with alarm.

'Let's see if someone volunteers,' I said, knowing very well that no one would volunteer, except maybe Charlie because she was nuts. There was no way I was pepper-spraying her in the face, even if she was the most annoying girl on the planet!

We were halfway down the stairs and Johnny J was tucking the pepper spray into his inside pocket when Rich appeared from nowhere.

'Volunteer for what?' Rich said, and my heart nearly fell into my stomach.

'Nothing!' I said.

'Helping with the old folks,' Johnny J said. *Good comeback*. I wished I'd thought of it.

Rich laughed. 'Yeah, right – old people freak him right out.'* He didn't believe us. 'Where were you?' he said, and he was pointing his finger in my face.

'Upstairs.'

'Liar.'

'Not lying.'

'I went up there. You weren't there.'

'Well, I was there and I'm on the stairs now. See?' I pointed to myself.

Rich looked confused. 'But I was up there,' he said, looking around. 'I didn't see you.'

'Well, I didn't see you either.'

'But?' Rich said.

'You need us for anything?' Johnny J said, helpfully moving us off-topic.

Rich nodded slowly. 'Come and listen to the band,' he said.

---

* 1. I trembled and vomited in my mouth when old people tried to touch me with their gnarly old hands.

2. My mother blamed it on the fact that we had no living grandparents. I'd never gotten used to wrinkles, weird smells or wonky parts.

3. When I was six, an old woman tried to shake my hand. I panicked and kicked her in the shin. My mam didn't allow me near old people after that.

'No. I'm busy,' I said.

'Wasn't talking to you. Johnny J, will you have a listen?'

We followed Rich down to the shed. Buzz, Fingers and Cap were practising their dancing.*

'All right, lads?' Buzz said.

'Good, thanks,' Johnny J said, and he leaned against the wall. I just stood there, not quite sure where to put myself. I'd never been allowed in the shed when the lads were practising before. They got in line and they started to sway even before they started singing, then they started clicking their fingers, even Fingers, which looked weird. I was mesmerised. Rich counted them in.

'One, two, three, four . . .' And they started to sing. They sounded like the vocal equivalent of nails on a chalkboard.

'Well?' Rich asked Johnny J when they had finished.

---

* 1. Buzz's real name was Ben, but his hair stood on end and people said it was because he was electrocuted when he was seven.

2. Fingers's real name was Justin, but he was born with only two fingers and a thumb on his left hand.

3. Cap was short for Captain America. His real name was Bradley. He was the only Bradley in Ireland at the time and it was an American name, hence Captain America/Cap. He had normal hair, all his digits and no spots, so he was considered the good-looking one in the band. Cap was the one all the girls would go for.

'Your harmonies are all over the place – it needs work,' Johnny J said. I just folded my arms and nodded along. I didn't know what harmonies were, but I could definitely tell that they were all over the place!

Cap gave Johnny J a dirty look.

'What does he know, Spots?' he said to Rich, who had so many spots on his face it looked like he had a chronic case of the measles. Fingers grinned madly. He looked all right except for his missing fingers, and Buzz, well, Buzz was from another planet, wearing pink cords and his mam's fur jacket. (He thought it looked cool. It did not.) He was really friendly but he freaked me out. I really wanted to get out of there.

'Any chance you'd play with us some time?' Fingers said to Johnny J.

'Sorry, I can't.' *He'd rather put his noodle in a blender. HA HA!*

'I think we'd sound great together,' Fingers said. 'We're working hard.'

'It's not that. I'm just busy.' *And he'd rather put his noodle in a blender! HA HA!*

Fingers nodded. 'Yeah, sorry about your mam.'

'Thanks,' Johnny J said, and he looked away.

He hated when people brought up his sick mother.

'Well, think about it, maybe when you have some time on your hands,' Rich said. 'We'd love to have you.'

Yeah, well, he'd rather put his noodle in a blender! SO BACK OFF! I didn't say it, I just thought it.

'Sorry, just really busy,' Johnny J said, and as we walked away, he mumbled, 'Your brother's a spacer.'

He didn't need to tell me. I already knew. We were halfway up the garden path and laughing at the notion of Johnny J singing with my spacer brother and his spacer friends when Rich stepped out of the shed and called me.

'Jeremy, wait up.'

Johnny J went into the kitchen and I turned back to my brother.

'What?'

He walked right up to me and whispered in my ear, 'You were in Rachel's room,' he said, and a little poo escaped.

'No, we weren't,' I lied, but my face turned red, then purple, and my eyes felt like they were bulging out of my head.

Rich grinned and nodded his head while pointing at my tomato face. 'Yeah, you were, and I'm trying to set up a gig. If I do, Johnny J is going to sing with us.'

'No way.'

'So I'll tell Mam.'

I could have threatened that I'd tell her about the stash under his bed, but he'd just get rid of it before she got home and I couldn't risk a war. If Rich told on me I'd be grounded for at least a week, and if I was grounded I couldn't rob Jim Roland's granny. All I could do was pray that no one in their right mind would give Fingers & the Fudge a gig before the end of the week. After that it didn't matter if my mam grounded me for life.

I relaxed a little – no need to say anything to stress Johnny J out any further. What were the chances?

9

The Pepper Spray

I loved the summer. Every day was a new adventure, some better than others. Most of them were spent in the forest, climbing trees, racing bikes, making swings out of tyres and old ropes, falling off those trees, racing bikes and swings, getting bandaged up in A & E and then returning to spy on unsuspecting teenagers and laughing. There was always lots and lots of laughter.

Johnny J and I arrived at our patch in the forest with the pepper spray in hand. Sumo was lying on the grass looking up at the sky. It was a sunny warm day and our giant friend seemed content. Walker, by contrast, was walking around in circles, pushing his glasses up his nose and mumbling to himself. He looked at his watch when we reached him.

'It's nearly 1 p.m.' He was really angry.

'Sorry, the key took longer to find than we thought,' Johnny J said.

I ignored him. Walker was nearly always late, it was no big deal, and anyway where else was he supposed to be? NOWHERE.

'Where's Charlie?' Johnny J asked. I really hoped she wasn't coming.

Sumo pointed to the sky. Johnny J and I looked up. She was hanging upside down and waving from a tree. Of course Charlie Eastman was hanging upside down from a tree – she couldn't stay upright and on the ground like a normal person. She started to climb down and Sumo got up. We stood in a circle.

'Well?' Charlie said.

Johnny J took the can of pepper spray out of his jacket and held it up.

'It doesn't look that scary,' Sumo said.

'Well, it's a can. Cans don't look scary,' Walker said.

'We just have to make sure that anyone who crosses our path understands how scary it is,' Johnny J said.

'So we think we should test it,' I said. 'Any volunteers?'

For once Charlie remained silent.

'I have asthma. There's no way,' Walker said, and to be fair, everyone agreed he couldn't do it.

'He's too weak,' I said.

'I'm not weak. I have a condition,' he said.

'Yeah, a condition that makes you weak,' Charlie said.

'Shut up,' he said.

I shrugged. 'It's just the truth.' That was probably the first thing Charlie Eastman and I ever agreed on.

I definitely didn't want to be the test dummy for the pepper spray, but I felt pressure to volunteer because it was my sister's pepper spray and it was all my idea. I was just about to put my hand up when Johnny J found his voice.

'It's for my mam. I'll do it.'

I didn't like the idea of Johnny J getting pepper-sprayed in the face. He had enough going on.

'You sure?' I said.

He nodded. 'It's the right thing to do.'

'OK,' I said, but I handed the can to Sumo. I just couldn't bring myself to spray my pal in the face. Sumo was gentle. He'd do it right.

73

Except he didn't do it right. He held the spray out in front of Johnny J with the nozzle facing the wrong way. No one noticed.

'Are you ready?' he asked quietly and calmly.

Johnny J gulped hard, squeezed his eyes shut and gave Sumo the thumbs up.

'Ready,' he said.

'OK, one, two, three . . .'

Sumo pressed the nozzle down. We were all staring at Johnny J, who was braced for pain, but none came.

'Well, that's not working,' Walker said just as Sumo let out an agonised scream and fell to his knees. The can hit the ground.

'My eyes, my eyes,' Sumo said, rubbing his eyes and almost immediately they swelled shut. He jumped up and ran in circles before slamming into a tree.

'Ah my face, my face . . .' he screamed, still pawing at his eyes and face. 'Everything burns.'

'What happened?' Johnny J asked me while grabbing Sumo and redirecting him away from the trees.

'He's after spraying himself in the face!' Walker said.

'I'm blind,' Sumo cried.* He fell to his knees, still holding on to Johnny J.

'What do we do?' Johnny J called out to no one in particular.

Sumo was rubbing his eyes vigorously now. They looked really sore.

'I'm guessing rubbing is not a good thing,' Walker said.

Johnny J held Sumo's arms away from his face. It was hard, Sumo was strong, but Johnny J kept repeating, 'It's for your own good.'

Sumo rolled onto the ground and Johnny J got on the ground with him.

'We need water,' Johnny J said, and Sumo nodded his head because he couldn't speak any more. He was deep breathing.

'The public loos are a three-minute walk from here,' Charlie said.

'So?' I said, and I felt really bad. Sumo was in an awful way.

'So we could shove his head down the loo,' she said.

---

* 1. His other symptoms included a runny nose, coughing and spluttering and a loss of coordination and balance.

2. At one point he made a miaowing sound like Mr Lucey's newborn kittens.

3. His mouth stayed wide open and in a circle for a really long time.

75

'You want to drown him?' I said in disbelief.

'No, idiot, the water will cool down his eyes.'

'That's gross,' Johnny J said. Those public loos were in a terrible condition.

'It could work,' Walker said.

'Sumo, do you want us to bring you to the public loos and shove your face down the loo?' Johnny J said.

'Yes, please,' Sumo gasped, and it should have been a warning.

It was a sign. We just ignored it.

10

The Public Poo

It took the four of us to help Sumo to his feet and then steer him toward the public toilets.

I checked the cubicles. The least I could do was find him the cleanest one. The good news was that it had been cleaned recently.*

'In here! This one is the best,' I said.

Charlie and Johnny J led a blind and gasping Sumo inside. Walker waited outside.† He couldn't

---

* 1. The bad news was that the porcelain was stained brown.
  2. Smelled like poo.
  3. And wee.
† 1. Walker called public loos public poos, and refused to go into them on account of them being full of nasty bacteria.
  2. He always did his business in his own house or in a bush.
  3. He was chased with his pants down by a fox once and it didn't change his mind.

watch it. I don't blame him. It was a hard thing to witness.

Sumo got on his knees. I lifted the toilet seat. He plunged his head down the toilet! He actually did it. I couldn't believe it. He rose up, drenched to the skin.

'Flush it,' he said, and he shoved his head back into the loo and Johnny J flushed it over and over again until eventually Sumo re-emerged.

'Enough,' he said, and he leaned against the wall. His eyes were still burning, but at least he could open them and he could breathe freely, which was a big relief. Walker thought it best that Sumo got fresh air into his lungs.

Later, we sat around the picnic table staring at Sumo eating a Spam sandwich he kept in his inside pocket for emergencies.

'I think that was the worst thing I've ever seen,' Charlie said.

Everyone was feeling a little low. I needed to do something to regain some control, so I stood up and addressed them: 'So the good news is the spray works. However, the bad news is we absolutely, definitely cannot and under no circumstances use it on Jim Roland's granny.'

They all nodded in agreement.

'So we absolutely, positively will only use it in emergencies and not on anyone over the age of sixty or under the age of ten,' I said.

They nodded in agreement again.

'We're going to have to hope Mrs Roland nods off,' I said.

'But what if she doesn't?' Walker said.

The public poos had given me an idea. 'She'll go to the loo,' I said. 'All old people pee a lot. Everyone knows that.'

'Fact,' Walker mumbled.

'So we stake the place out, and when Jim Roland's granny either goes to the loo or falls asleep, Johnny J and I will take the cash from the till. Charlie, you grab the petty cash from the back. Walker, you'll stay on lookout, and, Sumo, you'll stand guard at the door.'

'How do I alert you if someone is coming? Mind-melding?' Walker asked.

He had a point.

'What about our walkie-talkies?' Johnny J said. 'Perfect.'

'Walkie-talkies?' Walker said. 'I love walkie-talkies.'

79

'Great,' I said, and things seemed to be looking up.

Sumo didn't say much except for, 'I smell wee,' and then he warned us never, ever to tell anyone that he'd plunged his head into a public poo sixteen times in a row. We swore we wouldn't, but we lied. Eventually we told everyone.

Johnny J and I walked Sumo home. It felt like the least we could do under the circumstances.

'Thanks, Sumo,' Johnny J said at Sumo's front door.

Sumo hugged Johnny J, almost crushing him. 'Any time,' he said, even though he definitely didn't mean it.

Charlie was sitting on Johnny J's wall when we walked up the path.

'I thought you'd gone home?' She just wouldn't go away!

'Me ma is in there,' she said.

'Oh,' I said.

Johnny J sat on the wall beside her. I just stood there.

'She ate this morning,' he said. He was talking about his mother.

'That's a good thing,' she said.

80

'Yeah.'

I felt awkward, like I shouldn't be there, but Johnny J was my best friend, not hers.

'I should get home,' I said, but neither of them heard me because she was busy whispering in his ear. *Stupid, rude, silly girl.*

'I'll see you tomorrow,' I said, and I walked away, leaving Johnny J on his wall talking to Charlie about the things they talked about when I wasn't around. She never talked to me like that, but I didn't care. I didn't want to talk to her at all.

That night I lay in bed listening to Rich singing through the wall and worrying about the robbery. We only had two days to wait. After that, I told myself, it would all be over. Of course, in reality, the robbery was only the beginning.

11
The Bribe

It was the day before the robbery and I woke up to my mam shouting the same thing she shouted every morning.

'JEREMY! RICH! JEREMY! RICH! UP, UP, UP!'

I'd always be awake and ready to move, but my brother snored through her pitchy hollering every time. The world could cave in on itself and Rich would go down snoring. I jumped out of the bed and stretched.*

---

* 1. I had growing pains all the time because I was growing at a really fast rate.

2. My GP told me to stretch in the mornings and evenings to help with the pain. He was a football coach in his spare time so he knew what he was talking about.

3. Being short, Rich didn't need to stretch. That annoyed him.

I was mid-stretch when Rich bounded into my room. I was surprised to see him because usually I was halfway through my breakfast before Mam led him into the kitchen by his ear. He plonked himself down on my freshly made bed. Rich sitting on my bed irritated me, and he knew it; that's why he did it. He rubbed his butt cheeks into my sheets.

'Numbnutbutt.'

'What do you want, Rich?' I said, and I really wasn't in the mood. I had a lot on my mind.

'You need to cut your hair,' he said. 'It looks girly and stupid.'

I grabbed my band and put my hair in a knot and tied it. Then I shoved my favourite pen and pencil into the knot.

'You look like a piece of Lego,' I said. 'A boring, brown-vested Lego man.' Rich's hair was short and his head was a little bit square. He really did look like a stumpy, grumpy little Lego man.

'Shut up,' he said.

I could see I'd hit a nerve. *Nice.* That made me happy. *Now get off my bed.*

'So the good news is I've got us a gig.'

'When?' I said. If it was any time after the following night, we were safe.

'Mam asked Mr Cornally if he'd let us play in the pub after the match, so you better get asking because we need to get practising.'

I think I made a noise. I heard a groan. It was coming from my direction. My head suddenly ached and my stomach tightened! TOMORROW NIGHT!!!!

'Cornally's going all out. He's even bought a chip fryer! He's giving out free chips and sausages during the games. Cornally's is the place to be, Jeremy. Tell Johnny J it's going to be a packed house.'

I couldn't speak. I wanted to. I wanted to shout, 'NO. NOT HAPPENING. NEVER.' But I couldn't risk it.

'It's too soon,' I said, and I sounded hoarse.

'Well, he better get over here then and practise,' he said.

We were supposed to be scoping out the garage and practising robbing Jim Roland's granny.

'Johnny J's mam's sick,' I reminded him, hoping to appeal to his softer side.

He thought about that for a minute. 'We all have our problems,' he said. 'He's in the band for one gig or you're in deep trouble with Mam. You decide.'

Rich strutted out of the room. It was a bad start to the day.

It was raining. When it rained we met in the den.

Charlie was there. I realised I'd have to accept the fact that she was part of our group now. It was hard. *Stupid change.** She was sitting in my seat. *Annoying.* The sofa fit three, well, two and a half: Johnny J on the left, Walker in the middle and me on the right. Sumo had his own beanbag. It was the largest beanbag I'd ever seen. His mam had it made especially for him. He always had trouble getting out of it but he giggled to himself as though he enjoyed the challenge.

I looked around and there were no other seats. Walker threw me a cushion from behind his back and I sat on that.

'Are we practising this robbery or not?' he said.

'We are. Johnny J's not,' I said.

---

* 1. Mrs Murphy (my favourite teacher ever) left to have a baby. She promised the new teacher would be lovely. She was mean as a snake and made Sumo cry. Change sucks.

2. Colin Baker's the Doctor regenerated into Sylvester McCoy's the Doctor! Change sucks.

3. My local supermarket stopped selling 5-4-3-2-1s, the best chocolate bar in the whole world, in multipacks! My mother only bought chocolate in multipacks. Change sucks.

85

'What?' Johnny J said.

'Rich knows we were in Rachel's room. He's threatening to tell Mam. If he does, I'm grounded. If I'm grounded, we can't rob Rolands'.'

'What does that have to do with me not practising?' he said.

'Rich wants you to gig with them in Cornally's after the match tomorrow night,' I said, and as I was talking my voice screeched a little.

Walker laughed. 'They're spacers.'

'I'm not doing it,' Johnny J said.

'You have to,' I said.

'No way,' he said.

'You have to,' Charlie said.

He looked at her and shook his head and sighed. I couldn't believe she was agreeing with me and he seemed to be listening to her.

'You need to practise with them today and tomorrow.'

'I'm robbing Rolands' tomorrow,' he said.

'They'll stop to watch the match like everyone else in the country,' I said.

'Except us,' Sumo said. He sounded sad. It was sad.

'Except us,' I agreed.

Johnny J stood up. 'Fine,' he said. 'But I'm never, ever singing with them again.'

'Absolutely,' I said.

He left. I took his place on the sofa.

'What now?' Charlie said.

'Charlie, you pretend to be Jim Roland's granny.'

'Why? Because I'm a girl?'

'No,' I said. *Yes.*

'You be Jim Roland's granny,' she argued.

'I can't be Jim Roland's granny – I'm getting the cash from the till,' I said.

'Well, I'm getting the cash from the back room.'

She had a point. I stood up and handed Sumo one of his comics, rolled up.

'What's that for?' he said.

'Pretend it's the spray and stand by the door.'

'I'm not using the spray.'

'I know. Just hold this and stand by the door.'

He stood by the door.

I looked at Walker. 'You'll have to be the granny.'

'I'm the lookout,' he said.

'Yeah, well, you'll have to be the lookout as well.'

'Can't do both.'

'We're pretending, so pretend to do both.'

He reluctantly agreed.

This is it, I thought. *We're practising a robbery.* I fought the urge to cry. Instead I gulped and got on with it.

12

The Runs

What followed was two hours of practising/rehearsing/ playing/messing and time-wasting. Sumo fought off make-believe old men/young men/kids/women with prams/aliens/ogres and even a knight. He always shouted to them that he had pepper spray, but in none of the scenarios where he was forced to fight did he even pretend to spray the can. Walker decided that Jim Roland's granny was a pincher. When I tried to tie him up, he pinched me really hard and told me I was a cheeky pup in a croaky old voice. After that she was a kick-boxer, a stuntwoman and a ninja. It was really annoying. He made it impossible to tie him up with all his jumping around. We fought about it.

'Take it seriously!' I shouted.

'I am taking it seriously. I'm supposed to make it difficult,' he said.

'Yeah,' I said, 'but not impossible. She's an old woman – there's no way she can do the Karate Kid kick!'

Charlie picked up a book and threw it at Walker's head.

'Ouch!' he screamed, rubbing his head.

'Next time I'll knock your block off,' she said to him before turning to me. 'Now practise tying him up. You have to secure him without hurting him. She's an old woman after all.'

I nodded. It annoyed me that she was so bossy, but I was also kind of impressed. She went back to practising opening her dad's locked box. It was similar to the one in the back of Rolands'. She opened it, poured the money into a bag, ran to the door. She kept doing it over and over again. It was weird to watch. She seemed happy when she did it in less than ten seconds.

'Don't know about the rest of you, but I'll be in and out,' she said.

We split up at six. I walked up my road and saw Johnny J leaving my house with his guitar slung on his shoulder. I ran to catch up to him.

'How did it go?' I asked.

'I don't want to talk about it,' he said.

'OK.'

'You?'

'Well, if we get chased by aliens or Jim Roland's granny turns out to be a ninja it won't be a problem,' I said.

'Should I be worried?' he said.

'Nah.' *He should be.* I was. My stomach started to gurgle loudly. We both ignored it. 'We're going to meet in the forest after dinner, on our bikes, to cycle to Rolands' and back and time it.'

'Good idea. I'll be there.'

Rich had asked Johnny J to rehearse again after dinner, but Johnny J told him to stuff it, and as he had nothing to bribe Johnny J with, he smiled and told him he'd see him tomorrow morning. *Poor Johnny J.*

'Are they still as bad?' I asked when we got to his door.

He just shook his head sadly.

'See you later,' I said, and I ran home because I suddenly felt an intense need to go to the loo again! *Oh no!* I ran with my legs closed, knees together and my bum pinched tight.

'You all right, son?' my dad asked as I pushed past him in the hallway and held the seat of my pants as I ran upstairs.

'No,' I shouted. I tried to open the toilet door. It was locked.*

'Noooooooooooo!' I screamed. 'Get out, get out, get out!!!' I banged on the door with both my fists.

I could hear Rich laughing from inside the bathroom.

'Guts at you again, Jeremy?' he sang out sweetly as I banged and screamed and cried a little as I felt the red-hot lava fall into my pants and dribble down my leg.

'You better get up there, Debbie,' my dad shouted. 'Jeremy's destroying himself again.'

My mam was up the stairs like a bullet. 'Get out of the bathroom right this second,' she screamed at Rich. He opened the door, smiling. I stumbled in, pulling at my trousers. My mam stood outside while my insides fell into the toilet. The smell was horrendous. Trying to take my jeans off without

---

* 1. In the 1980s in Ireland most homes only had one bathroom.

2. Toilets, sinks and baths came in putrid green, pale pink and dark brown. We had a pale pink bath and a putrid green sink and loo because my dad got them cheap.

3. Everyone I knew had carpet on their bathroom floor. Think about it, soaking into the carpet!

92

getting poo on my legs was horrific. I was crying loudly by the time I was showering it off. All the while my mam was outside the door saying things like, 'OK, son, you're all right now, Mammy's here. No panic.' At one point she sang 'You've got a friend', which was her favourite song to sing at parties. When I appeared in the doorway, she took one look at me.

'You're very pale.' She felt my forehead. 'You don't have a temperature.'

'I'm fine,' I mumbled, conscious that my dirty jeans and pants were in the bath. I tried to wash them but I kept gagging.

'Are you stressed?' she said, and I couldn't admit to that because if I did she'd ask me why I was stressed and I'd crack and tell her everything.

'No. I think I ate something bad at Sumo's,' I said.

'Not that Spam rubbish?' she said.

'Yeah, Spam,' I lied.

'Oh God!' she said. 'Go to bed. I'll open a bottle of 7Up.'

'Ah no, I'm grand,' I lied, genuinely fearing my own death. The stuff that came out of me!!!!

'You are not grand,' she said, marching me to

my bedroom. 'But don't you worry – everything will be fine. Some flat 7Up will sort you right out by morning.' In case of emergency, my mother always kept an open bottle of flat 7Up in the fridge.*

I couldn't go to bed and drink flat 7Up all night. I had to meet the lads in the forest and time a test route to Rolands' Garage, but my mam had me in my pyjamas before I could argue and tucked up in bed sipping flat 7Up. Escaping from my room would be as hard as escaping any jail in any country in the world. It was a disaster!

---

* 1. Lots of mothers back then believed that flat 7Up could cure anything – bad stomach, a cold, flu, a broken leg, a missing toe.

2. Anything that happened to any kid out on our road and you could hear the twist of a cap and the escaping fizz before their front door had closed.

3. To my knowledge, there is no medical proof to the theory that flat 7Up is a cure-all, but it tasted aces.

13

The Escape

The hall phone rang. Mam shouted from the kitchen for Rich or my dad to answer it, but they were stuck to the sofa, shouting at the telly, and it kept ringing and ringing. Eventually she answered it.

'Hello, the Finn household, who's speaking, please?*

'Ah there you are, love.' I could tell it was Rachel on the phone as soon as my mam picked up. 'How's nursing? . . . Oh good. How's the lovely boy you're with? . . . I know his name is Rupert, Rachel . . .

---

* 1. There was only one phone in every household and it lived in the hall.

 2. When you answered it, you didn't know who was calling you. It could have been anybody!

 3. Kids had to ask permission to use the phone, and when the phone bill came, dads went nuts and kids scattered!

95

I do know it. Dear God, I didn't know it was a test!'

My mam and Rachel had a very odd relationship. They totally idolised and annoyed each other in equal measure.

This went on for a while, my mam asking my sister about what she was doing, where she was going, if she was remembering to wear her coat even though it was June.

I lay in bed listening to every word spoken, because back then the walls were paper-thin and my mam had a voice that travelled. I was in a panic, trying to figure out how to escape, but my mam's loud voice kept interrupting my thoughts. Then she mentioned Mrs Tulsi and my heart started to race.

'Oh, Rachel, love. She's not good. She's not good at all.' Then she was crying again, big loud sobs. 'They say she'll be lucky if she lasts the summer. Ted's devastated. He doesn't know what to do. And that sister of hers, well, you know what she's like. She's on her way over.'

There it was – the worst news I'd ever heard in my entire life. All of a sudden I had a pounding headache and my hands were sweating. *Oh no, oh no, oh no.* I wanted to headbutt a wall, stamp my feet, shout, shake, jump up and down. I wanted to run, punch, kick, scream. Instead I crawled into my bed and under the covers and had a little cry until my mam hung up the phone.

After I'd wiped away my tears I focused on the task at hand. I needed to make my escape and fast. It was still bright and sunny, so my mam had closed the curtains to allow me to sleep. I grabbed my old Mickey Mouse watch. It was just after 7 p.m. I had less than thirty minutes to escape my house and run to the forest. The forest was twenty minutes by bike, and my bike was in the back garden and impossible to get to unseen. I really didn't know how long it would take to run it. I'd never done it before. My guts screamed, my head ached and my eyes burned, but I was determined.

I fixed the pillows to look like the shape of a human boy under the covers, then I peeped outside my bedroom door. The area was clear, so I tiptoed into the hallway. I was halfway down the hall when I heard the toilet flush, so I shuffled backwards to my room, closed the door quietly and leaned against it, listening for the toilet door to open and close. My dad whistled as he left the loo and then burst into a sea shanty halfway down the stairs. I waited until I couldn't hear him any more and then I ventured out of my room once again. I looked left and right. It was clear. The bathroom door was open, so no surprises would come from there. Rich was caterwauling in the garage and Rachel was miles away in nursing school, so that only left my mam. I wasn't sure where she was. My heart raced as I crept down the stairs. The sitting-room door was closed. I could hear Johnny Giles on the telly. He was talking about the England–Netherlands game and my dad was laughing.

'You're right, Johnny. God Almighty, never a truer word spoken,' my dad shouted to the TV. The kitchen door was open and I could hear my mam pottering around in there from my position (I'd pretty much painted myself against the wall) on the stairs. The kitchen was at the end of the hall, which meant with the door open my mam had a direct line of sight. Blood pulsed through my veins at an alarming rate.

As soon as I heard the kettle go on I knew I needed to make a run for it. She'd have her back to the door if she was making tea. I grabbed my jacket and I opened the door ever so slowly and carefully and I inched around it and closed it ever so quietly. I felt the fresh air hit my face and tasted freedom and I ran as fast as my feet could carry me.

The boys and Charlie were sitting around the picnic table, waiting for me. It was 7.40 p.m. when I got there. I'd run all the way.

'What took you so long?' Walker said, and he was annoyed.

'Sorry, I had to escape, Mam put me to bed, it's a long story,' I said in between wheezes and holding my stomach tight so whatever was left in it wouldn't try to escape.

'You don't look well,' Charlie said.

'Yeah, well, I've just run a marathon,' I said. 'I'd like to see how you'd look.'

'Easy,' she said. Now I was annoyed.

Sumo sat on the ground eating a Spam sandwich. The smell of it made me queasy. *Keep it together, Jeremy.*

'Where's your bike?' Johnny J asked.

'The back garden,' I said, and everyone stared at me. 'I couldn't get it without being seen.'

'So how are we supposed to plan our route if you have no bike?' Walker said.

'I'll just get on the back of one of yours,' I said.

'You should cycle Walker's, with him on the back,' Sumo said.

'Good idea,' Walker said. 'My asthma's really playing up.' It wasn't. He was just lazy. I'd been hoping for a rest after pooing my guts out and running five miles.

Everyone got onto their bikes. We all stood in a line – Johnny J, me with Walker behind me clinging on a little too tightly for my comfort, Sumo next and at the end Charlie. She was the only one with a basket in the front. So we agreed she'd take the bags.

'Ready?' I said.

'Ready,' they said, and we were off.

14

The Rehearsal

We started cycling. It took exactly ten minutes from the forest to Rolands' Garage along the main road, cutting through Pearce Estate and over the bridge. When we got there, we parked our bikes behind a large container on the wasteland opposite the garage and hunkered down behind a grassy verge. Walker had binoculars he'd borrowed from his dad's bedroom. He put them against his face and started telling us everything that we could already see.

'Right, Roland's in there and the oldest son – you know, the one with the ronnie and the bad teeth.'*

---

* 1. Ronnie is the Dublin slang word for a moustache.
  2. People said Roland's son grew it to cover his rotten teeth.
  3. It didn't hide them. It framed them.

'We're only across the road, Walker, not a mile away,' Charlie said.

He ignored her. 'They're laughing about something. Ronnie McBadteeth is eating a chocolate bar.'

'Wow, that's very helpful,' Charlie said. She could be very sarcastic.

He ignored her.

'Walker, check out those cameras,' I said, pointing to the two cameras facing the petrol pumps. 'Are they fixed or do they move around?'

'Good question,' he said, and he focused the lens and looked. 'Nah, no swivel on them. They're going nowhere.'

'So if we come and go from the shop side, they won't get us on camera,' Johnny J said.

'Yeah,' he said, 'and I have a clear view of the entire street from right here. I can tell you if anyone is coming before they even hit the forecourt.' Walker seemed happier about things. He focused the binoculars and pointed toward the public toilets. They were around a corner, so he couldn't see anything really. He took the glasses away from his face. 'How long do you think it takes a granny to pee?' he asked, and Sumo made a face.

'It takes my granny ages,' Charlie said.

'Mine too,' Walker said.

'How long do you think we'll need to grab the money out of the tills and the back?' Johnny J asked.

'Ten seconds,' Charlie said, 'and we've practised tying up the granny just in case she doesn't go to the loo.'

Johnny J wasn't comfortable with that at all. We argued about it. I warned him we only had the time it took to play a match to get this done. If she had a strong bladder and we didn't have a back-up plan, we were done for.

There was a lot of talking and arguing about that, and then Walker called for us to shush. 'Ronnie McBadteeth is on the move.' I looked at my Mickey Mouse watch* and counted the seconds between him walking from inside the shop, outside to the courtyard and then around to the toilet.

'Ten seconds exactly.' Then we all waited, with me studying the second hand of my watch moving and counting, twenty seconds, thirty . . . fifty . . .

---

* 1. No, I didn't like Mickey Mouse.
  2. It was a communion present when I was seven.
  3. The few times I ever wore that watch involved robbery.

103

one minute . . . one minute ten . . . twenty . . . I carried on with everyone watching until he emerged at just over two minutes and fifteen seconds. Then we counted the extra eleven seconds it took him to walk from the toilet back into the shop and behind the counter.

'That means we have two minutes twenty-five seconds, loads of time,' I said.

Walker corrected me. 'We have two minutes – cut the time it takes to come and go. We don't want to meet them on our way in or out.' He had a point.

'It will take a granny a lot longer to get from the loo and back,' Charlie said.

'That's if she goes at all,' Sumo said.

Then we argued again over tying up a granny. Johnny J said he'd rather not do the robbery than lay a hand on the lady. I agreed it was difficult. I wondered if he knew what I knew, that without America his mum wouldn't last the summer. I didn't say that though. I didn't know how to and I didn't want to. I couldn't face it. We finally agreed that the robbery would only happen if the woman went to the loo. That's when Charlie suggested that she bring some of her mam's special home-made lemonade and sold it to her for 10p.

'Why would someone in a shop buy lemonade from you?'

'Well, first of all, it's delicious, and secondly, I'm cute – she thinks I'm lovely, and I'll pretend it's in aid of the local football team.'

'That's brilliant,' I said before I knew what I was saying.

'It is brilliant,' Johnny J said.

'I AM BRILLIANT,' Charlie said, and in that moment she seemed less brilliant.

So the new plan was that Charlie would go into the shop with a bucket of free lemonade for Jim Roland's granny, then change behind the big bin on the wasteland back into her Ireland gear, but instead of face paint she'd put on her brother's Darth Vader mask. After we'd agreed the new element of the plan, Johnny J ran across the road and stood outside Rolands' with his walkie-talkie and I hid behind the verge with mine and we tested whether they worked.

'Testing one, two, three. Are you there, Number One Buddy? Over?' I said.

'Loud and clear, Brown Bear,' Johnny J said.

The others looked at me.

'Brown Bear?' Charlie said, and Walker and Sumo started to laugh. I blushed red.

'It's a code name,' I said, 'and anyway it's cool.'

'No, it's not,' she said, but I ignored her. I didn't care what Charlie Eastman thought.

When Johnny J returned, we redrafted the plan for the one-hundredth time. We got back on our bikes and separated, cycling as fast as our legs could carry us. Johnny J was to take the same road back, Walker and I cycled down Clyde Road, crossed over the tracks and through Leonard's Park, Sumo went through the Barns Road estates, but because there was a massive wall that separated the estate from the road, he threw his bike over it and climbed it. He arrived at the picnic table first. Charlie took the back roads by the canal. She came in last, but only because she met her mother on the road and she sent her to get a batch loaf. Johnny J arrived second and I got there third. I think if I wasn't really sick and carrying Walker I would have come in second. Either way, we were all back in the park within twenty-five minutes. If we planned the robbery for the start of the match, that gave us all plenty of time to escape, hide the money and slip into Cornally's pub before the match ended.

It was perfect. As we parted we knew the next time most of us would see each other we'd be robbers.

'Scared?' I said as we all gathered in a circle around the picnic table. Everyone nodded. Everyone was scared.

'We'll be OK,' Walker said. 'We can do this.' He had been the most against the plan, so it was comforting to hear that from him.

'Let's do this,' I said, and the others mumbled, 'Yeah.' It wasn't convincing, but I didn't push it.

Johnny J took me home on the back of his bike. We didn't talk – there was nothing else to say. When we arrived at the gate, I walked up to the door and put the key in the lock, holding my breath. No one in the hall, no one on the stairs. I closed it quietly and crept into my room, stripped off, jumped into bed, and when my heart stopped racing, I said a little prayer. 'Please, God, please let us get away with robbing Rolands' Garage and get enough money to save Johnny J's mam. I promise I'll never, ever do another bad thing. Thank you, all best, Jeremy. Oh, and Mary, Mother of God, if he's not inclined to help, have a word, please. Thank you, all best, Jeremy Finn, over and out.' I was so tired I don't remember anything after that.

15

The Lies

I spent the next morning helping my mam clean the house; I vacuumed the downstairs hall and carpet, dusted the sitting room and cleaned out the cooker to ease my guilty conscience. My mam was happier with my colour and she was sure the flat 7Up had sorted out whatever illness I was battling, but she was still determined to keep a close eye on me. *Just my luck.*

'Are you positive you won't watch the match with us in Cornally's?'

'We're watching the first half at Sumo's. Maybe we'll come for the second half,' I said.

'You know they're doing free chips for everyone.'

'Yeah, I know, but it'll be packed.'

'Sure isn't that half the fun?' she said pleasantly, before sighing sadly and hitting me where it hurts. 'It's a special day, son. We've already lost Rachel. We should be together.'

'We haven't lost Rachel, Mam.'

'Well, she's not here, is she?' she said.

I felt really bad. My mam always had a way of making me feel like I was doing something wrong if I wasn't doing what she wanted me to do. 'We'll definitely come for the second half,' I said, and she seemed happy enough with that.

I arrived at the den just after 2 p.m. Kick-off was at 4 p.m. Sumo was alone when I got there. He was playing a game of Space Invaders. I just stared at the screen. For ages we didn't talk; we just sat together and yet alone all at the same time. Sumo's mum broke our comfortable silence.

'Ah there you are, Jeremy,' she said after she'd knocked three times and Sumo called out for her to enter. She was holding a plate of Spam sandwiches.

'Hiya, Mrs Lane,' I said.

'Would you like some sandwiches?' she said.

'No, thanks, Mrs Lane.'

'How's your mammy?'

'Great, thanks.'

'And your daddy?'

'Good too, thanks.'

'And Rachel? Is she still at nursing school?'

'Yeah.'

'And she's still dating the doctor?'

'His name is Rupert.'

'Like the bear,' Sumo said.

'He wears a scarf too,' I said.

'Is it yellow?' Sumo asked.

'No,' I said.

'Your mammy must be very proud.'

'She is,' I said.

'Are you coming inside for the match?' she said, and Sumo stopped playing his game and just sat there and waited for me to answer.

'We were going to watch it in Cornally's pub with my parents,' I lied.

'Ah lovely,' she said. 'We're having the McQueens over and the Simpsons. I'll be doing sausages and burgers. We're going to make an evening of it, so you and your parents are more than welcome to join us after the match.'

'Thanks, I'll say it to them,' I lied again.

'Right so,' she said, and she put down the plate

110

of sandwiches beside Sumo, who sat still, like a statue. She walked out and closed the door behind her.

'What are you thinking?' I asked him.

'Dunno.' He shrugged. 'Just feeling bad about missing the match.'

'Yeah, me too,' I said.

Sumo turned to me. 'Even if we get in trouble, it will be worth it, won't it, Jeremy?'

'I think so,' I said.

'Even if no one can fix Johnny J's mam, at least we tried,' he said.

I nodded, even though the thought that even if we succeeded it might not mean Johnny J's mam's survival had never crossed my mind. *Ah no. That's not going to happen.*

'That has to mean something, doesn't it?' he said.

I nodded. *SHE WILL SURVIVE. SHE HAS TO. I'M NOT LOSING MY BEST FRIEND TO HIS AUNTIE ALISON AND ENGLAND!*

Sumo sighed, sniffed and then picked up the joystick and killed another bunch of plodding aliens.

The others arrived a while later and suddenly the once quiet, tame room was alive with voices and nervous energy. Walker was pumped. Within two minutes he was dressed in his green shorts and T-shirt. He painted his own face with a green, a white and a yellow stripe. The face paint was really thick on his face. He paced the room like a panther, waiting for it to dry, almost walking a hole into the floor.

'Are you nervous?' Sumo asked him.

'I don't do nervous,' he said.

'I'm nervous,' Sumo said.

'Yeah, well, don't be,' Walker said. 'Nerves get people killed!!!!'

We were in various states of undress and we all stopped what we were doing.

'No one is going to kill us, Walker,' I said.

But Walker wasn't listening.

'We need to set our watches to the same time,' he said.

'Why?' Johnny J asked.

'I dunno – they do it on the telly,' he said.

'I'm not wearing a watch,' Charlie said.

Walker stopped dead. 'Ah no, how are we supposed to rob a place when this one can't even be bothered to put on a watch?'

'We're going together – there is no need for a

watch,' Johnny J said while trying to get his leg in a pair of green shorts that he chose to wear over his jeans. Johnny J didn't do shorts.

'I don't know, lads, this is feeling very unprofessional,' Walker said.

Charlie ignored him. She had been busily painting the Irish flag on Sumo's face, but she was done, and when he turned toward us, it was weird – the flag on his face did make him momentarily unrecognisable.

'That's good,' I said. I didn't mean to give her a compliment. It just slipped out. I don't think she heard me though because she was too busy attacking Walker.

'If you want to weasel out, Walker, just do it,' she said, and that really annoyed Walker.

'Who are you?' he shouted at her. 'Since when are you a part of anything?'

To be fair to him, it was a good question.

'Leave her alone,' Johnny J said, but Charlie didn't need Johnny J to defend her.*

'I'm Charlie Eastman,' she said, 'the girl who's

---

* 1. The word on the street was that her rugby-playing older brothers, Louis, Sean and Ben, were afraid of her.

2. I used to think it was a joke.

3. After spending time with her I began to think that it might be true.

113

robbing a garage this afternoon. Who are you?'
She was very cheeky but was funny too.

Walker scowled. He wasn't used to anyone
putting him in his place. He didn't know what to
say, which made a nice change. Walker usually had
the answer to everything.

Johnny J laughed out loud. I laughed inside.

'Well?' she said. She wasn't letting Walker off
the hook. 'Who are you?'

Everyone immediately looked to Walker. He
shrank back a little. 'Yeah . . . eh . . . erm . . . I'm
a garage robber too.' He was unconvincing if I'm
honest, but he was trying his best, and when it
looked like he might cry, Sumo walked over to him
and punched him in the arm (lightly – if he had
put some welly into it, Walker would have died).

'It's OK to be nervous,' Sumo said.

'I AM NOT NERVOUS,' Walker said, fixing his
glasses on his flag face and pushing Sumo away.
Sumo just sniffed and went back to his game of
Space Invaders.

Charlie painted all the rest of our faces. She took
longest painting Johnny J's. It made me want to
puke. (Not really – my stomach felt surprisingly
good.) Then we all put on the red beards and the

big hats, except for Walker, who just kept touching his hairsprayed quiff and talking about, 'Not the hair, no way, not the hair.' Sumo wore a wig. The rest of us didn't bother because it was really hot.

16

The Photo

It was a beautiful afternoon, the sky was a light, bright blue and the sun shone down, hot against our painted faces. We stood all together in Sumo's garden in a circle. We could hear the TV inside the house, blaring pre-match analysis, and there was Irish music drifting down the street. Above us, a bird was squawking loudly and we just stood there in a circle, five green-white-and-gold-bearded football-fanatic-looking leprechauns.

'Everyone knows what they have to do,' I said.

Charlie and Johnny J said, 'Yeah.' Walker and Sumo just nodded.

'What time is it?' Charlie asked.

Walker pointed to her. 'You see?' he said. 'Watches are important. FACT.'

Just as he said it, the squawking bird pooed on his shoulder.

'Ah nuts,' he said, and we all laughed, even Walker. We probably only laughed for a minute or so, but it seemed much longer at the time.

'Charlie, do you have the Darth Vader mask?' I asked.

She pointed to it, sitting alongside a long cotton dress and a large flask of her mam's famous home-made lemonade in the basket of her bike. Johnny J gave her the thumbs up and she blushed.

Before we had a chance to leave, Mrs Lane came at us with a Polaroid camera.*

'Gerry,' she said. 'Gerry, would you come out here?'

Sumo's dad popped his head out the door. He was drinking from a can of beer.

'Would you look at them?' she said, pointing to us five demented-looking, flag-faced, orange-bearded weirdos.

---

* 1. Camera phones didn't exist.
 2. Most cameras had film in them that had to be developed and that could take up to a week.
 3. The Polaroid camera was the only instant camera on the market. It was state of the art back then.

117

'God Almighty, lads, you're all out. Ha!'*

Mrs Lane insisted on us lining up in front of her so she could take the snap.

'Take off the beards – I can't see your lovely smiles,' she said, and we all dropped our beards around our necks.

'Ah lovely, say *cheese*,' she said, and we all said, 'Cheese.' She took the photo, and when it popped out of the camera, she handed it to Mr Lane, who fanned it while she took another one.

'Another cheese for me, kids – and, Jeremy, give me the thumbs up.' I did what I was told and we all said, 'Cheese,' again, and by the time that photo was taken, the first one had developed in Mr Lane's hand. He peeled off the cover and laughed to himself.

'Ha, spot on, Mary, that's a keeper. Yerrah, that's one for the wall in work,' he said. That meant he liked the photo.

We didn't wait around to see it. We had somewhere to be.

'Enjoy the match, boys,' Mr Lane said, not realising one of the flag-faced leprechauns was a

---

* 1. Sumo's dad was from the country.
2. Country people say weird things like 'Ha' and 'Yerrah'.
3. I don't know why.

girl. Even though she would be wearing a mask, Charlie had insisted on getting her face painted, to be like the rest of us.

'We will, thanks, Mr Lane,' I said. The others waved at him and it was time.

We took off on our bikes, and as we made our way there, the streets became emptier and emptier. Everyone disappeared inside their homes, the homes of friends or neighbours or filed into the pubs. The bunting still fluttered above us, the flags flapped from upstairs windows and car aerials, but the excited chatter quietened, the music and electric excitement faded from the streets. That joy and thrill were somewhere else now, in rooms with flickering TVs. We wouldn't be a part of it.

For the first time, I felt really, really sad about that, but I didn't say anything. None of us did. We just took it all in as we cycled the empty streets.

'I'm really sorry,' Johnny J said.

'It's no big deal,' I said, but it was a big deal. The greatest thing that had ever happened to Ireland (at least according to my dad) was happening right then and there and we were missing it, but for something way more important: Johnny J's mam.

119

By the time we reached the wasteland opposite Rolands', it was four minutes to kick-off. Walker looked through the binoculars and confirmed that Jim Roland's granny was sitting behind the counter, even though we could all see her. She wasn't as fragile as I'd hoped. She looked tall and strong, and even though her face was wrinkled and her hair was grey, she was broad and solid. Maybe she was a ninja after all.

Charlie put on the big old cotton black dress covering her football gear and took out the lemonade. 'I'm going in,' she said.

'Good luck,' Johnny J said.

She walked across the empty road and straight into the station. We watched her ply Jim Roland's granny with 10p lemonade.

'Well, she's thirsty enough,' Walker said from behind his binoculars. 'She's drinking like a horse.'

Ten minutes later, a pint of the best lemonade Jim Roland's granny had ever drunk and a chat about how brilliant the girl scouts were in the 1920s, and Charlie was back beside us, with the black dress off, an empty flask and her Darth Vader mask hanging from her neck. All we had to do was wait.

17

The Robbery

Jim Roland's granny must have the strongest bladder in the history of bladders. It was thirty minutes into the game and she hadn't budged. I was starting to panic.

'Maybe she never goes to the loo. Maybe she's a robot!'

'She's not a robot,' Walker said with great authority. 'If she was I'd know. Fact.'

'We need a distraction,' Charlie said as she put on her Darth Vader mask.

'What kind of distraction?' Walker asked.

'We could kick out one of the exposed pipes and flood the loos?' she suggested. That idea sounded pretty sinister coming from Darth Vader.

'Oh, right, you mean add destroying property to the many other criminal acts on our ever-growing CV,' Walker said. 'Maybe we should just set the place on fire while we're at it.'

'OK, maybe you're right,' she said. 'I've a better idea.' *Of course she did.* 'One of you tell her there's a leak in the toilet. When she goes to investigate, we'll lock her in there.'

'How?' Johnny J said.

'There's a key for the toilets beside the till. Roland locks them up every night so that poor people or freaks don't move in and live there.' It was a good idea. Charlie Eastman was born to be a criminal.

'Live in a public poo?' Walker said, aghast.

'Yeah,' she said, nodding sadly. 'Some people have terrible lives.'

Living in a jail cell must be as bad if not worse than living in a loo, I thought. My stomach started to churn. *Pull it together, Jeremy!*

'I like it,' Johnny J said before he looked to me. 'Well? Jeremy? What do you think?'

'Yeah,' I said, 'it's good.' At that point anything was better than hiding on a grass verge with paint melting off our faces on account of the unusually hot sun. Besides, it was a good plan. In fact, it was deadly. I really wished I'd thought of it.

'So who's going to tell her the toilets are broken?' Charlie asked. She couldn't, for obvious reasons.

'I'll do it, Vader,' Johnny J said, and Charlie grinned. She liked being called Vader. That was something to worry about as far as I was concerned.

'No,' I said, 'I'll do it.'

But Johnny J fought me. 'It's for my mam, Jeremy.'

I nodded. 'OK, here's the new plan: Johnny J goes into the garage and tells Jim Roland's granny the loos are leaking. He brings her across to the toilets. As he's moving around to the back of yard, Vader and I move in. Vader grabs the key and gives it to me, I run around and pass the key to Johnny J so he can lock Jim Roland's granny in the loo and Vader grabs the money in the till and the money in the back room of the shop.'

'What about me?' Sumo said.

'You're still on the door.'

'That's it?'

'That's it.'

'And Walker?'

'He's still on lookout here.'

123

'All right then,' Sumo said, before confirming, 'I just stand there at the door.'

'Yeah, but you'll have the spray and the walkie-talkie. If Walker alerts you that some big burly man is on his way in before we're done, you have to spray him.'

He nodded as he felt the can in his inside pocket, but it was clear he was not happy. 'It's so mean,' he said under his breath.

'Remember to spray him, not yourself,' Walker added, and laughed to himself. No one else laughed. We were too nervous. As we were leaving I handed Walker the walkie-talkie.

'Good luck,' he said, before adding, 'Do not mess this up or I will kill you.'

He was serious. I believed him. If any one of us could be a killer, my money was on Walker.

As I scrambled over the grass verge and crossed the road to Rolands' Garage, I remember thinking, *This is it. After today I'll be a robber.* My heart sank in my chest and I really, really wanted to cry.

Walker tested the walkie-talkie set as we made our way across. Despite making fun of us he must have liked the idea of code names, because he came up with two very quickly.

'Cash, this is Tango, do you receive? Over.'*

'. . .'

'Cash? Come in, Cash.'

Sumo stared at the walkie-talkie before pressing on the button. 'Hello, Tango, er, this is Sumo. I think you've got the wrong number.'

Walker sighed deeply. 'This is Walker. Tango is my handle, Cash is yours. Over.' I want to say I thought the handle names Tango and Cash were uncool, but I can't. They were very cool. I was beginning to regret Brown Bear.

'Oh,' Sumo said, but he looked confused.

'Just answer to Cash. OK? Over,' Walker said.

Charlie, Sumo and I waited around the side of the garage. She held the three bags, one inside the other, while Johnny J led Jim Roland's granny out of the garage shop and around the back to the toilets.

From across the road and lying on the grass verge on his stomach, Walker watched us all through the binoculars and held the walkie-talkie close to his lips. 'The Eagle has landed. Over,' he said.

---

* 1. *Tango & Cash* was a huge movie in 1989. Certificate fifteen. We weren't allowed to watch it, but the trailer rocked and Walker had the poster on his wall.

2. Sylvester Stallone played Tango. Walker was no Sylvester Stallone.

3. Kurt Russell played Cash. Sumo was no Kurt Russell.

125

'What eagle?'

'Oh, come on, Sumo. The granny is in the loo. Over.'

'The granny is in the loo,' Sumo repeated, and Charlie and I ran as fast as our legs could carry us into the empty shop. Sumo stood at the door, holding the can out, like a gun in a gangster film. Charlie grabbed the key from beside the till and threw it to me. I ran out and handed it to Johnny J, who stepped away from Jim Roland's granny, who was bent over the toilet.

'I can't see anything, love.'

The door slammed and Johnny J turned the key, locking the door.

'Eh, I think the door is stuck, love. Love? Eh? Hello? Love? The door might be stuck?' Jim Roland's granny started banging on the toilet door as we ran into the shop.

Charlie had already emptied the till into her bag. There wasn't enough cash in the till to fill one bag. She ran to the back room.

At the door, Sumo bounced up and down in one spot like he was desperate for the loo. 'Any sign of anything, Tango? Over,' he said, and Walker responded.

'All clear, Cash. Over.'

Sumo kept checking the can to make sure that it was pointing outwards and not toward his face.

I followed Charlie into the back. The cash box was open, so she didn't need to break into it, but there wasn't that much money in it. Just a few fifty notes, a couple of twenties and some tens. Nothing like the amount we'd expected. She stuffed it in the bag and handed us the two empty bags. Then Charlie looked at me, and even though she had a Darth Vader mask on, I could tell she was scared. I saw actual fear in her eyes.

'If we leave here with this money, there's no going back. We're robbers,' she said, and I gulped hard, my stomach flipped and I nodded. Tears filled her eyes. 'OK,' she said.

'OK,' I said, and I wanted to hug her, but just for a moment. On the way out she didn't lift up the countertop. Instead she just jumped over it. *Show-off.*

127

18

The Getaway

As we reached the exit I looked around. 'Where's Johnny J?' I asked Sumo.

'He's watching the granny,' Sumo said. That was not part of the plan and I was a bit miffed.

'Come on, let's go,' Charlie said.

Just as we were leaving, Sumo's walkie-talkie crackled to life.

'Tango, come in Tango?'

Sumo fiddled with the controls of the walkie-talkie.

'Hello, Cash. Over?' he said, and Charlie raised her eyebrows, which really annoyed me. Sumo wasn't the one jumping over counters.

'Eh . . . Johnny J is being chased around the forecourt by Jim Roland's granny.'

We all looked out the window. 'Ah no!'

I heard Walker say, 'Cash out,' but I was already running to Sumo, who was now just standing at the door watching a granny chase Johnny J around the petrol pumps.

'What are you doing?' I said to Sumo.

'I'm not spraying a granny,' he said, and he shook his head from side to side.

I grabbed the bag of money from Charlie, shoved it into Sumo's hand and shouted, 'You and Walker just go.'

Sumo threw the pepper spray up in the air and was off and running before I'd even finished the sentence. 'We are on the move, Walker – I mean, Cash. Let's get out of here,' he said into the walkie-talkie as he ran from the garage.

'Copy that. Over,' Walker said. I could see him hang his binoculars around his neck, pocket the walkie-talkie and then the two of them got on their bikes and cycled off in separate directions. I don't know if Jim Roland's granny even noticed that Charlie/Vader and I were there, because she was so focused on Johnny J. He was pinned behind petrol pump no. 3. We needed to do something, and I had a plan.

'You go. I'll distract Jim Roland's granny. See you later,' I said to Charlie.

'Are you sure?' she said, and I was sure. She needed to go.

'Go.'

She ran off across the road to pick up her bike and scarper as I ran up to the granny and tapped her on the shoulder. She turned around and eyed me up and down. Then I ran and she turned her back on Johnny J, just long enough for him to slip away from the pump he'd been cornered behind. It was then I saw a car roll into the garage and a man got out of it.*

Jim Roland's granny saw the same man and screamed, 'Help! Help me.' Then she pointed to Johnny J and me. 'Bad boys,' she screamed, and when he looked my way, I nearly browned myself.

'RUN!' Johnny J shouted, and so I ran as fast as my legs could carry me, off the forecourt, across the road, where I picked up my bike, jumped on, and with Johnny J right beside me, together we cycled down Clyde Road, crossed over the tracks

---

* 1. He was tall.
  2. He was huge.
  3. He had fists the size of dinner plates.

130

and sped on into the forest. We kept looking back to see if we were being chased, but the Giant and Jim Roland's granny were far behind us. We pedalled like we'd never pedalled before, eventually making it to our spot. Walker, Sumo and Charlie were waiting. I practically fell off the bike. My legs were shaking. Johnny J just stopped and stood over his. I think he was in shock.

They had the bag of money in front of them. Walker was writing down figures on a piece of paper. No one looked happy.

'Are you OK?' Charlie asked Johnny J.

He nodded.

'What about you, Jeremy?' she said, and I nodded.

'I'm OK,' I said.

She looked from us to Walker. He pushed his giant heavy glasses up on his face.

'How much?' Johnny J asked.

'Not enough,' Walker said, and Johnny J and his bike sank to the ground. 'There's two hundred and sixty-five quid there,' Walker went on. 'With the money we earned off the boxing, our combined pocket money for this month and the tenner Sumo's Auntie Julie gave him, that makes a total of five hundred and twenty-seven pounds, fifteen pence.'

We were all quiet for a long minute. Finally Johnny J spoke. 'How much more do we need?'

'At least another five hundred, if we want return tickets, taxi fare, a few quid for the hospital shop while she's there – you know, for grapes, magazines, 7Up.'

We all stared at him. 'Who cares about magazines and 7Up?' Charlie said.

'Eh, sick people,' Walker said. 'And besides, I've only allocated fifty quid for that – the rest is plane and taxi fares.'

Sumo checked his watch. 'We need to go, lads,' he said.

We left our bikes in the bushes and hid the bag of money in our secret spot before walking to Cornally's. No one spoke. We were all pretty deflated. We had tried but we had failed.

We entered through the back of the pub. All eyes were on the TV screen and the place was jammed with people; no one really noticed us. The game was in its seventieth minute and the people gathered were mesmerised. We just stood there and watched the Irish team play the last few minutes of mediocre football. It was as though nothing had happened, like we'd been there from the start. When the game ended at 0–0, some people groaned, others clapped a little and everyone started to look and move around. The pub emptied a bit – not much, but I saw my parents and waved over. Mam was delighted to see me.

'Ah, son, I didn't spot you there.'

'Yeah, Sumo's was boring. It's better here.'

'Ah yeah,' she said. 'The chips were lovely, weren't they?'

'Yeah,' I said, and my stomach grumbled. I was starving.

We got seats when a family of twelve left. Mr Cornally decided that the atmosphere wasn't conducive to a boy-band performance and cancelled the post-football gig. It was the only real bright spot in Johnny J's day.

When I went to the loo, Walker grabbed me on my way in. He held my arm. He seemed anxious. I knew the feeling – it was why I was trying to reach the toilet.

'So we'll wash cars or we'll sell some of Charlie's mam's lemonade – that stuff's amazing. Have you tasted it?' he said.

I shook my head. I had not. 'We don't have that kind of time,' I said.

'Look, I know she's given up the chemo, but that doesn't mean she's just going to die. She could be grand for ages,' Walker said.

'She won't last the summer,' I said.

Walker let me go. 'What?'

'Johnny J's Auntie Alison is coming to get him. We did it all for nothing. It's over, Walker,' I said, and then I went into the toilets, into the stall, closed the door, sat on the loo and cried.

19
The Gurriers

The morning after the robbery I walked into the kitchen in time to hear Mam and Dad discussing the Rolands' robbery AT OUR BREAKFAST TABLE!

'How many of them were there?' my mam was asking as I entered the kitchen.

'At least two, maybe three,' my dad said.

'Poor Nellie,' my mam said.

I grabbed some toast and said nothing.

'She's some woman,' my dad said. 'She was out of that back window like Jack Flash and chasing the little gurriers off.'* I'd never been called a

---

* 1. Jim Roland's granny's name was Nellie.
  2. There was a large window in the Rolands' public loo that Charlie hadn't thought to mention.
  3. The definition of a 'gurrier' in the dictionary is a tough or unruly young man.

gurrier before, at least not that I knew of. I didn't like it.

'How much did they get away with?' Mam asked. I sat next to her, facing my dad and trying my very best to butter my toast without giving away that I, Jeremy Finn, was one of the gurriers they were speaking of and a fugitive from the law. *Be cool, Jeremy. Just be cool.*

'Could have been thousands,' my dad said. *Eh, no, Dad, not even close!*

'And they found pepper spray at the scene,' my mam said.

'Pepper spray?' my dad repeated. 'What is the world coming to?'

She shook her head. 'Some people really are disgraceful,' she said. *Eh, it's your pepper spray, Mam!* I thought. I did not say anything.

'Is the lady all right, Dad?' I asked, and my dad looked at me and smiled.

'Yeah, son, she's fine. She just got a fright, that's all.'

'A fright at her age could kill her,' my mam said.

'Well, it didn't,' my dad said. 'Still, it was a terrible thing to do, and when Ireland were on the field! Desperate times,' he said sadly. He shook his head from side to side and sighed.

My mam nodded along. 'I hope they do time,' she said.

I felt sick again.

'You OK, Jeremy?' my mam asked, feeling my forehead.

'Yeah,' I said.

'How's that stomach of yours?'

'Grand,' I said, but it was doing somersaults again. I left before she could put me back to bed.

It was another really warm day, blue skies and birds singing. I could feel the burn through my clothes as I walked into the forest. Walker was already there, sitting on the bench and using his inhaler.

'Stupid allergies,' he said, before blowing his nose and examining the contents of the tissue. I sat down beside him on the bench and leaned on the wooden picnic table, resting my head on my hands. We didn't talk, he just spun his inhaler on the picnic table and I closed my eyes and listened to birds chatter above us. Johnny J and Charlie were the next to arrive. Sumo was last to the table. He squeezed in beside Walker and Charlie. Johnny J was next to me. I raised my head. Walker stopped spinning his inhaler and we all faced one another. We talked about the robbery and about how scared we were.

'When I saw the man, I weed myself a little,' Sumo admitted.*

'When I went to check on Jim Roland's granny and she jumped out the window at me, I nearly died!' Johnny J said.

'Running out of the shop with the bag of money, my knees wobbled all the way to my bike,' Charlie said.

'Cycling away from the scene, the fastest I've ever cycled in my life and terrified I was going to have an asthma attack,' Walker said.

'Cycling away for me too, terrified we were being followed! It was the most scared and excited I've ever been, just like a roller coaster.' The word 'gurrier' rolled around in my head.

'Except for it not being legal,' Charlie said. 'A roller coaster may land in you in hospital, but not in prison.'

'Yeah,' I agreed. Everyone talked about how

---

* 1. I also peed myself as I cycled down the Clyde Road.

2. I cried a little, passing over the tracks.

3. And I had to physically cover my mouth with my hand to muffle a scream as I reached the forest.

buzzed they were during the robbery. Nobody said how depressed and sad they were when we all realised that we hadn't scored enough money.

'What now?' Charlie said.

Johnny J shook his head. 'Nothing. We should just give the money back.'

Walker stood up. 'We're not doing that,' he said. Everyone looked his way. 'We have to do it again,' he said.

'No,' Johnny J said, shaking his head from side to side.

'We can't,' I said. I couldn't imagine going through all that again. 'I can't even think of where. It's just impossible.'

'I can,' Walker said, and he started to pace around the picnic table as he spoke. 'You know that my dad drives the money van for the bank?' He stopped walking and looked at us all.

'So?' Charlie said.

He started circling again. 'So he keeps a spare set of keys to the van in the house. Usually there's three of them – my dad drives, a big fellow called Tom goes into the bank and collects the money, and there's another little fella, they call him Titch, he stays in the back of the van. He takes in the

139

money and secures it in a safe built into the floor. While my dad's in Italy at the matches, they can't find a replacement, so Tom is driving *and* collecting the money and Titch is still inside the back of the van.' He stopped.

'So?' Charlie said again.

He took off again. 'So I know the code for the van depot. We could let ourselves into the van. When the little fellow jumps in, we can tackle him and tie him up.'

'What about Big Tom?' Johnny J said.

'He drives, collects, pushes the money through a slot; he doesn't go near the back of the van. When Tom collects the money and pushes it through, we grab it and as soon as we've got enough – one bag should do it – we wait till he stops at traffic, jump out and make a run for it.'

I couldn't believe what I was hearing. 'Have you fallen on your head?' I asked, because that's what my dad asked me every time I did or said something stupid.

'I'm deadly serious,' he said, and he stopped moving and finally he sat down.

'But you're too smart to go to jail,' Charlie said sarcastically, but Walker was serious.

'Is her dying a fact?' he asked quietly. He didn't make eye contact with Johnny J, but I did. He looked like he was going to fall apart into a million pieces.

'Fact,' I whispered, and the word burned in my throat.

'We have to save her,' Walker said, and he shrugged. 'We just have to.'

I didn't want to do it. I didn't have the stomach for it. I wanted to cry. I wanted to run away.

20

The Mastermind

No one spoke. We all just sat at the picnic table for what seemed like a really long time, lost in our own thoughts and fears. Finally I gulped and said what I felt I had no choice but to say.

'OK.' I didn't want to do it but I had to.

I looked around the table. Sumo and Charlie nodded. 'Yeah,' Sumo said. 'I'm in,' Charlie said.

Johnny J couldn't speak. He was battling hard to hold back tears, fighting with his own insides.

'How are we going to get into the depot unseen?' Charlie asked, diverting attention away from him.

Walker fixed his glasses to his face and held them there as he spoke. 'The security guard leaves at

5 a.m., the lads come in for 6 a.m. We have an hour to get in and hide before they arrive.'

'Where do we hide?' Sumo asked.

'There's a storage area where they keep all the mops and cleaning stuff. No one goes in there but the cleaning lady, and she's only in on a Monday and Thursday night. None of the men ever go there.'

'And when do we slip into the van?' I asked.

'The lads do a walk-around as soon as they get in. Then they go for a coffee and a smoke, and that's when we get into the back of the van.'

Sumo put up his hand. 'What's a walk-around?'

'It's when they check the van for any damage, make sure the back is empty and stuff,' Walker said.

'How are we going to keep the little fellow quiet?'

'We're going to gag him, tie him up and threaten him with pepper spray, and this time if we need to use it, we will.'

No one argued, not even Sumo. I was shocked.

'Are you serious?' I asked.

'Deadly,' he said. I couldn't believe it. He was a criminal mastermind and it was terrifying.

'Who's going to drive the van if the driver runs away?' Charlie asked.

'Why would the driver run away?' I asked.

'He might be scared,' she said.

'He won't even know we're there,' I said.

'But if he does?'

'We're kids – he won't be scared. We'll be scared.'

'OK then – he opens the van, we spray him in the face with pepper spray. He can't see to drive, we need to get away and it's too dangerous on foot. Who drives?'

'It's a stupid question!' I shouted.

'No, it's not,' Walker said. 'We need to think about every eventuality.'

'I'll drive,' Johnny J said, and we all looked at him. 'If I have to drive, I will. I move cars in my uncle's garage all the time,' he said.

'Yeah, from one car space to another in a yard,' I said.

'So? Driving is driving,' Walker said.

'No, it isn't,' I said. Johnny J knew how to change gears, accelerate, brake, turn and stop. That's it. He had never actually been in traffic or driven around a roundabout and he didn't have a driving licence.*

---

* 1. Being caught for robbing is worse than being caught for driving without a licence.

2. Being caught for robbing and driving without a licence is worse than being caught for driving without a licence or robbing alone.

3. Being armed with really sore pepper spray while robbing and driving without a license was worse than . . . (Well, you get it.)

144

'Of course it is,' Walker said.

I looked to Johnny J. He nodded.

'It's OK. I can do it.'

'Good,' Walker said. I let it go.

'When?' I asked.

'Three days' time,' he said.

'The Ireland versus Netherlands game? But that's at eight o'clock at night.'

'I know,' he said.

'So you want us to rob during the day, while the match isn't on to distract everyone?' I said.

'My plan doesn't need the match to distract everyone because we'll be hiding in a van. Besides, even before the match comes on, people will all be distracted, waiting for the match to start, and half the country will still be decked out in the Ireland gear all day, especially the kids, so it's good cover.'

He was right. It didn't matter if it happened during the match or not, and the best bit was that if we did make it through the robbery undiscovered we could watch the match! *Hurrah! Finally a light at the end of a very dark tunnel.*

'Anyone got any objections?' I asked. Everyone stayed silent.

'OK then, it's decided. We'll hijack a cash van,'

Charlie said, and it sounded so insane we all started to laugh, even Johnny J. Of course we were terrified. We knew what we were doing was highly dangerous, but we also knew that after we did this one last robbery we'd never have to do another one.

'There's thousands in those vans. Fact,' Walker said.

'We'll just take enough to make up the difference,' Johnny J said, and we all agreed that was the thing to do. I was amazed that Charlie and Sumo were on board when they didn't even know about Auntie Alison coming to snatch Johnny J away from us. It was brave and they were good friends, even if she was still really irritating.

After we'd agreed to hijack and rob a cash van we played football for the rest of the evening. It was brilliant fun, the lads and Charlie running around, using coats for goalposts under a pink sky. Above our heads the birds were swooping, diving and singing a loud song. The ice-cream van's jingle wafted through the air, and for a really short time life was really, really good and I forgot we were gurriers.

21

The Hummingbird

It was nearly teatime when we parted at the forest gates. Johnny J and I cycled together, only getting off our bikes at the top of our road. We always got off our bikes there and walked the last stretch of the journey.

'Do you think we can pull it off?' Johnny J asked.

'We pulled off robbing Rolands',' I said.

'Yeah, but this is big stuff – we're robbing a security van! "SECURITY" being the important word in that sentence.'

'But we have a code and a key and an evil genius in our friend Walker,' I said.

'Do you think I can drive that van if I have to?' Johnny J looked worried.

I'd thought a lot about that since Walker had suggested it, and I believed he could, because Johnny J could do whatever he put his mind to. 'Yeah, you can do it. Besides, it won't happen like that. We'll just grab the first bag that comes through the slot and jump out as soon as the van stops at a light. Easy,' I said.

'How do we get home?' he said.

'We'll catch the bus.'

'With a bag of stolen money?'

'Yeah,' I said. 'It's a gym bag – people will think it's smelly gym gear. Who'd want to take that?'

He laughed. 'You're my best friend in the world,' he said.

'You too,' I said.

We didn't look at one another. It was embarrassing. He just nodded and I nodded and then he punched me in the arm and then I punched him. We had just reached his house when a big black taxicab drove onto our road, passed us and stopped right in front of Johnny J's. My heart squeezed in my chest as the blonde woman dressed head to toe in black stepped out. I knew who it was even before she turned around. I heard Johnny J gulp and I felt a searing pain in my chest as my heart broke in two.

'Auntie Alison,' he said. She didn't hear him – she was too far away and busy wrestling her large suitcase from the taxi man's hands. We both stopped walking and just stood together, frozen.

She stood in front of the house, staring up at it before looking around the street, and that's when she saw us. She broke into a smile and waved. 'Johnny.'

Johnny J just stood there, petrified to the spot. She dropped her case and walked over to him as quickly as her really high heels would allow. She hugged him tightly and then she ruffled his bouncy hair. Johnny J stood still, with his hands by his side, not moving, not speaking. I looked on in horror.

'There you are, my poor, poor boy,' she said. 'Don't worry – I'm here now. Auntie Alison will take care of everything.'

She looked around at me. 'You're the friend,' she said.

'My name is Jeremy,' I said. 'Jeremy Finn.'

'Do you know what I do for a living, Jeremy Finn?' she asked. I did know. Auntie Alison had a string of hairdressers' across the UK. She was very successful. She was very wealthy. She was used to living in a better place than our little street and being around more successful, richer and no doubt smarter people than us, at least that's how she made us feel.

'I know what you do,' I said.

'Well then, I'd be happy to give you two boys a free haircut,' she said.

I really didn't like Auntie Alison at all.

She looked back at the front door of the house again. 'I should go in,' she said.

Johnny J didn't move.

I nodded. 'Yes,' I said.

She walked back and picked up her case. 'Right then, in I go,' she said, but she didn't move. It was like being surrounded by living statues. I waited. She just stood there, her suitcase in hand. Then the front door opened. It was Uncle Ted. He stood still, holding on to the door and looking at Auntie Alison. For the longest time nobody moved or spoke. It was freaky. Finally Uncle Ted nodded and Auntie Alison started to move toward him. When she reached the door, she handed him her suitcase. She walked past him and he closed the door. It was a big relief.

'Are you OK?' I asked.

'No,' Johnny J said, shaking his head.

'Me neither.'

He didn't want to go inside, so we sat on the wall. I think he was in shock. Auntie Alison's arrival was news to him. I hadn't told him I'd overheard my mam talking to Rachel about it. I regretted that. Maybe if I'd warned him, he wouldn't be shaking. I offered him my coat. He shook his head again.

'I think it's over,' he said, but just as he said it a bird swooped down right in front of our faces. It flew up, then down, then backwards and upside down, its pretty, colourful feathers and long, tapered bill mesmerising us. I could hear the humming coming from its flapping wings. Unmistakable.* There was a hummingbird hovering right in front of our faces and I swear it was looking us straight in the eye. It was remarkable.

'I spy, with my little eye, something beginning with *h*,' I said.

'Hummingbird,' Johnny J said, and his eyes lit up and a smile crept across his face.

---

* 1. When Johnny J had his appendix out aged six, his Auntie Alison bought him a book on birds. It should have been boring but it was brilliant.
  2. Johnny J and I read that book front to back and back to front, one million times, and birdwatched for an entire year before we discovered video games.
  3. WE KNEW OUR BIRDS!

'What did that book say about spotting a hummingbird?' I asked, pretending to forget.

'It said that when a hummingbird hovers nearby, it means you are capable of achieving the impossible,' he said.

'Everything's going to be all right,' I said, and he nodded, because *h* is for hummingbird but it's also for hope.

22
The Fear

In the two days after Auntie Alison's arrival, life became more difficult. Walker was the only one who seemed happy about planning a new robbery. He kept promising us that it would work and that everything would be fine. I wanted to believe him but I couldn't. Jim Roland's granny had almost caught us. Now we were planning on sneaking into a security warehouse and jumping into a van unseen, overcoming a grown man (I didn't care how small he was) and stealing bank money. That made us bank robbers. This was not good. It was not good at all.

Every time I closed my eyes I had a terrible nightmare. I was trapped in a box or a cage or underwater or in a bin or under a bed. Once, I was stuck in the U-bend of a toilet. That was the worst. I forced myself to stay focused on the fact that Johnny J and I had seen the hummingbird. Whenever my faith wavered I thought about that. *We can achieve the impossible!* Then I thought, even if we did achieve the impossible and we got the money, sent Mrs Tulsi to America and saved her life, it still didn't mean we wouldn't get caught. Seeing a hummingbird did not mean you'd never go to jail. I tried to think of anything else we could do to get the money to save Mrs Tulsi and avoid spending the rest of my life sharing a very small room with bars on the windows with a boy called Stab-a-Rasher for a cellmate.

Johnny J was nervous too. In a bid to avoid robbing a security van, he tried to sell his guitar, a speaker and his bike by putting notices up in all the local shops, but no one came knocking.* Charlie said everyone was too absorbed in the football to buy things. She was probably right. But I hoped he could, because I really didn't want to

---

* 1. Johnny J's guitar was so old it had a hole in the side, which he covered with gaffer tape.
  2. His speaker crackled.
  3. The bike was missing one handlebar.

rob a cash van. His mam was spending more and more time in bed, and he sat by her bedside playing games of I spy and talking about their favourite things. One of the days, I called in to pick him up for rehearsal with my stupid brother. Uncle Ted let me up the stairs. Mrs Tulsi was so small in the bed I couldn't really see her under the mountain of covers. Johnny J sat on the floor, his back resting against the bed frame, but his hand was raised and his mam was holding it tight. They were mid-game so I just stood in the doorway and kept quiet.

'My favourite ice cream is rum raisin,' Mrs Tulsi said.

'Chocolate chip,' he said.

'My favourite superhero is Batman,' she said.

'Superman,' he said.

'My favourite time ever is the day I had you,' she said.

'Me too,' he said, and I heard her cry out a little, and he turned and gave her a kiss on her cheek and fixed her blankets the way my mam fixed mine.

'It's going to be all right, Mam, I promise,' he said.

Johnny J accepted that nobody wanted to buy his second-hand stuff quickly enough, so when he wasn't with Mrs Tulsi he was either planning the robbery with Walker or practising in the band with my brother. He couldn't quit rehearsals as long as we needed to keep Rich quiet.

I missed my friend. I was also anxious all the time. Everyone was talking about the match, my brother's stupid gig or the robbery, and so I spent most of my time battling stomach pain and running to the nearest available toilet.

My worst moment was when I heard Mr Lucey talking to my dad about the Rolands' robbery and how the police thought it was boys from a local rough estate.

'Really?' my dad said.

'Sure who else would it be?' he said.

Eh . . . me! I thought.

'I hear they threatened to give her a kick,' Mr Lucey said. *WE DID NOT!*

'Animals,' my dad said.

'I heard the guards raided a few houses last night. It was a big operation, Ron,' Mr Lucey said.

'Go on!' my dad said, and I had to clench really hard to hold my insides in! 'They broke down the Fitzers' door,' Dad went on.

'No!' Mr Lucey said.

That was it, the moment I made a weird sound I'd never heard from myself or anybody else. Mr Lucey and my dad looked around at me.

'Are you all right, son?' Dad said.

I nodded, but I wasn't all right at all – that was Freaky Fitzer's mam and dad's door they broke down! He was a bully, but he didn't deserve that.*

'Word on the wind is they didn't find Roland's cash,' my dad said.

Of course they didn't – my friends and I had it! The local newspapers had carried loads of stories about it. One of the articles featured a comment by Jim Roland's granny. 'I'm not the same since,' she said.

It was terrible to read. I thought I'd be sick. I was still off my food and my mam wasn't happy.

'Maybe I'll take you to the doctor.'

'I'm fine, Mam.'

'I'm not sure you are.'

'I am. I'm just not hungry.'

I heard her talking to Rachel on the phone. 'He's

---

* 1. I heard later that Freaky Fitzer's dad stood in his garden in his boxer shorts, a pair of white socks and brown sandals.

2. Freaky's mam kept pointing the finger at Freaky and saying, 'I'm going to kill you.'

3. Freaky shouted at his mam that he was running away and then he didn't.

157

losing weight, and the smell in the bathroom after him. It would burn the eyes out of your head.'

'MAM!' I said, and I could hear Rachel laugh at the other end of the phone. I left when she started talking to Rachel about the robbery. I couldn't listen to it any more. Jim Roland's granny's words – 'I'm not the same since' – really played on my mind. *What if we'd ruined her life?* It was a huge burden. *What if we do succeed in robbing the security men and they lose their jobs? What if they can't get any other jobs? What if their families end up starving and homeless?* I had started something that I couldn't stop. I was trapped. I was tormented.

23

The Question

On the night before the Ireland–Netherlands match, Johnny J asked me to eat dinner at his house. By that point I was so sick and so scared that despite the hummingbird, or maybe because of it, I decided I was going to tell him I just couldn't rob again. Auntie Alison cooked spaghetti bolognese. Uncle Ted read the newspaper. Johnny J and I watched some of the highlights from Italy v Czechoslovakia and Germany v Colombia on the telly. When dinner was ready, Uncle Ted went upstairs (on Auntie Alison's instruction) to bring Johnny J's mam down for dinner. Auntie Alison directed Johnny J and me to the table and it took ages before Uncle Ted arrived down with Mrs Tulsi. She saw me and smiled a big wide smile. Uncle Ted was holding her up, keeping her close. She had a scarf on her head and you could see she was completely bald under it. Her eyebrows were gone too, but she still had those big watery grey eyes that Johnny J had and his Auntie Alison did too. She was really thin, but the veins in her arms and hands were fat and sticking out.* It was shocking. I wanted to cry. I closed my eyes and remembered how she used to look.

'I haven't seen you in months, Jeremy, and look how you've grown.' Her voice sounded different.

I couldn't talk, so I just nodded and messed with my ponytail.

Uncle Ted helped her to her chair. She sat beside Johnny J. She gave him a kiss on the cheek, and when her hand dropped under the table, I saw him reach for it and they sat beside one another quietly holding hands, but only for a few seconds.

'What's this?' she said to Auntie Alison.

'Spaghetti bolognese. It's good for you, so just try to eat some,' Auntie Alison said.

---

* 1. When she put her hand on my head and stroked my ponytail, her touch sent shivers down my spine.
  2. I felt really scared.
  3. And really ashamed of myself.

'Very fancy,' Mrs Tulsi said, and Uncle Ted laughed.*

'Nothing but the best for our Alison,' he said, and Auntie Alison just gave him that look, the one my mam gave my dad when she was unimpressed with him.

'And why not? Don't I deserve the best?' she said coldly, and Uncle Ted shut up and ate. Mrs Tulsi ate a few bites and everyone praised her.

'Lovely,' she said. 'That must be the first meal I've had in a good while.'

'Five weeks, Mam,' Johnny J said.

Uncle Ted ruffled Johnny J's hair.

Mrs Tulsi asked me about my plans for secondary school.

'I'm going to Luke's cos that's where Johnny J is going.' That wasn't strictly true. I was really going there because my brother went there, but I just wanted to make a point. Everyone stayed quiet, but Mrs Tulsi looked sad, Auntie Alison looked annoyed, but then she always looked annoyed, she had that kind of face, and Uncle Ted smiled and winked at me.

---

* 1. Italian food was considered fancy.
  2. French food was seriously posh.
  3. Mexican food was unheard of.

The spaghetti bolognese was probably the best spaghetti bolognese I'd ever eaten, but I was still glad to go. After seeing Mrs Tulsi I couldn't tell Johnny J I wasn't going to do the robbery, though by that point I was such a mess I wondered if they would be better off without me.

Auntie Alison told Johnny J to be home by 10 p.m.

'Don't go too far,' she said.

'I'm only going to Jeremy's,' he said.

'Well, make sure you don't go any further. Until they catch those thieves, you wouldn't know what you'd find yourself up against,' she said.

Johnny J blushed red. I wasn't sure if he was embarrassed because he was one of the thieves she was talking about or if he was annoyed that she was acting like she was his mam already. *Mind your own business, Auntie Alison!*

I tried to be cool, to remain calm and pretend. I wasn't very good at it and my friend knew me well. He could see I was panicking.

'You're still with me, aren't you, Jeremy?'

'Of course,' I said, and I meant it even if it killed me.

Johnny J spent the rest of his evening rehearsing

162

with the band. It was their third night practising in a row. If Johnny J was honest with himself he was starting to enjoy it, and if I was honest with myself they were starting to sound a lot better. Now that Johnny J was playing with them they dropped the backing tracks and he played guitar.

Rich was on a high. 'We're going to be the next U2,' he kept saying, and I felt sorry for him, because Johnny J made his band good and Johnny J was only there for one gig. This time next week we'd probably either be in prison or Johnny J would be in England living with Auntie Alison. So that last night, while Johnny J lost himself in his guitar, playing and singing sad songs about roses, thorns, cowboys, I wrote a letter to God.

Dear God,

I hope you are well. This is Jeremy Finn here. I confess that I have sinned. In my thoughts (I planned a robbery) and words (I talked about it too), in what I have done (I robbed a granny) and what I have failed to do (I failed to get enough money to send Johnny J's mam to America). And I'm doing it again, all of it – planning, talking, robbing and hoping not to fail again. I'm asking for forgiveness for what I've done and what I'm about to do, and I'm begging you to help us save Mrs Tulsi. You can put us in prison if you really feel you need to punish us. I understand we are committing very big sins, but please, God, save Mrs Tulsi.

Thanks very much,

Jeremy.

PS Please make me better at maths.

PPS And help me fit into my new secondary in September. (If I'm not in jail.)

PPPS And if my dad could win the Lotto, that really would be brilliant.

I folded up the letter and put it under my mattress for God to find.

After that I covered my head with my pillow and thought about the kind of letters I'd write home from prison.

'Dear Mam, I used to like bunk beds. I don't any more.'

'Dear Mam, my new cellmate is called Stab-a-Rasher. I'm really scared.'

'Dear Mam, I miss food.'

'Dear Mam, I miss you.'

I cried myself to sleep the night before we robbed Walker's dad's security van, and in the weeks and months that followed I realised I wasn't the only one.

24

The Hiccup

I told my mam that the lads and I planned to cycle to the beach and spend the day there. I said I'd be up and out before the rest of the house got up for breakfast. I didn't say I would be leaving at 4.30 a.m.! She didn't ask and was happy enough about it. She liked it when I was out of the house, and she also thought getting up early was a healthy and good thing. My nerves were gone. I was a shuddering, shaking wreck of a boy, but I was trying my best. As I was lying to her and she was smiling at me and reminding me to take the sun cream just in case the sun came out, I realised I might never speak to her again without the presence of a police officer or prison guard, so I hugged her tightly and held on, even when she rubbed my head, and I hated when she did that.

'Everything's OK isn't it, Jeremy?' she said.

'Everything's fine, Mam,' I lied.

'I know you're worried about Johnny J and his mammy,' she said, and tears sprang into my eyes because, yes, I was worried. I was worried all the time.

'All we can do is help them, the best way we can,' she said, and she was right. That's what I was doing, helping my friend and his mam in the best way I could. That thought got me out of bed at 4.30 in the morning, it helped me get dressed, and then I packed the Ireland gear and the stupid face paint in my backpack just in case we didn't make it home in time to change before the game. I crept down the stairs, jumping over the two middle creaking steps, and ran out my front door without making a sound, even though my hands and legs were shaking so much my bones rattled!

Johnny J was sitting on the wall waiting for me. He was pale and his hair and eyes were bigger than usual, making him kind of mad-looking.

'OK?' I asked.

'I threw up,' he said.

I hadn't. I had nothing left in me.

Charlie cycled to meet us. She was red-eyed. I think she'd been crying, but when Johnny J asked if she was OK, she smiled and said she was great. We just nodded, even though we knew she was lying. She was trying her best. We cycled to Walker's. He and Sumo were waiting there. His dad's work was a fifteen-minute cycle from Walker's house. We cycled in silence.

It was 4.59 a.m. when we arrived. We ditched the bikes in some bushes and Walker took out his trusty binoculars as we hunkered down behind some thorns. A lot of 'Ouch' and 'MOVE OVER!' followed. Walker told everyone to 'SHUSH.' We did, even though we were lying in thorns.

He watched the building and we waited. The security men left at 5 a.m. on the dot. They both got in separate cars and they drove in separate directions.

'Let's go,' Walker said, and we all stood up, slowly and painfully.

Sumo had a thorn sticking right into his cheek. He didn't seem to notice. Charlie pulled it out and showed it to him.

'Cool,' he said.

We followed Walker through the hole in the fence that he knew was there. He said his dad always complained it needed fixing. Sumo didn't fit through. Walker ran around to the gate and opened it for him. We walked up to the door, and that's when we heard the dogs, barking and snarling.

'Dogs!' I shouted.

'Big dogs,' Charlie shouted.

'They'll kill us all,' Johnny J shouted.

Sumo ran into a wall, trying to escape. Walker just laughed.

'It's a recording they put on to frighten anyone off,' he said. 'There's a lot of minding in real dogs.' He pressed the numbers on the keypad. The door made a buzzing sound. He pushed it hard. It opened and we were in.

The place was empty of people but full of vans and the sound of vicious dogs barking. It was dark and terrifying.

'Follow me,' Walker said, and we walked in line behind him. Johnny J, Me, Charlie and Sumo, each one of us holding on to the person in front of them. Walker tried to put the key in a van to open it. It didn't open. He went down the line, trying to open each van with no luck.

'Do you not know your dad's van?' Charlie asked.

'They all look the same, not to mention it's dark,' he said.

It was a good point. The fourth van he checked was his dad's van. It clicked open. He opened the back door and revealed the inside. As soon as Titch opened the doors he'd see Sumo standing there with pepper spray, and Johnny J and Walker standing behind him. Sumo was there to hold down Titch, Johnny J to take in the money through the slot and Walker because he knew how to open the double-locking system in the back of the van. Charlie and I were to follow the van on bikes. Johnny J kept one walkie-talkie. I had the other. Charlie and I needed to stay close enough to them to keep in touch – anything over ten metres apart and the walkie-talkies were useless. It was our job to tell the boys what was happening in the outside world, because there were no windows in the back of the van. We needed to access escape routes and alert them when it was the best time to jump out and make a run for it. Ideally we were looking for somewhere where they could jump out undetected and just blend in as quickly as possible.

In the cold light of morning our plan was already

in trouble. If Titch saw the lads just standing in his van, he'd run and shout for help.

'Sumo needs to get out of the van,' Charlie said as she walked over to some security uniforms hanging in an open wardrobe against the wall. She picked up a large uniform.

'Where do I go?' Sumo asked.

'Put this on and sit in the corner, keep your head down, don't talk to anyone,' Charlie said.

She turned to me. 'Change of plan,' she said. 'I can see the whole floor from the top window over there.' She pointed as she spoke. I looked up. She was talking about a second-floor window.

'Eh, how do you get up there?' I asked.

'There's a tree right beside it,' she said, and she said it in a tone that suggested I was stupid.

'I'll keep watch, and when Titch approaches the van, I'll radio Sumo, and, Sumo, you walk over and as soon as he opens the door you push him in. Johnny J, be ready to gag and tie him up immediately. Sumo, jump in straight after.'

Johnny J nodded.

'I don't want to hurt him,' Sumo said.

'We push each other all the time – do we get hurt?' Walker said.

'No,' Sumo said.

'Exactly,' Walker said.

Sumo nodded to himself and eyed the suit and grinned.

'That will work,' Walker said. 'As long as you don't mess it up, Sumo.'

Sumo hunched. 'I'll do my best.'*

---

* 1. It was a bad plan.
  2. It was a terrible plan.
  3. It was the worst plan in the history of bad and terrible plans.

25
The Wait

The plan had changed. It was sink-or-swim time. I felt like I was drowning.

'You'll have to stash all five bikes,' Charlie said.

'Impossible to cycle and hold four bikes. I'd have to walk. I'd never make it back in time,' I said. When we'd practised cycling, we only had five minutes to spare.

Walker thought about it. 'There's a bike stand at the library. It's just down the road. Put them in that and we'll grab them later.'

I agreed to stash three bikes at the library, and I'd leave Charlie's and my bikes outside and wait for her in the thorns.

First, Walker had to spray the back door of the

van with a little black spray paint so Charlie and I knew which one to follow. He did that. Then Charlie and I walked the lads as far as the cleaning room. Johnny J was worried that Charlie would get caught up the tree.

'Adults never look up,' she said.

'But you'll have to come down at some point,' I said.

'And when I do, I'm a little girl waiting for her dad,' she said, and she batted her eyelids, and when she did it she seemed really innocent.

We left the boys hiding in the cleaning room and Charlie climbed the tree while I hid the bikes in plain sight in front of the library and waited in the bushes with the backpack. I could see Charlie in the tree, looking through the window, but nothing else. So I just sat there. WAITING!*

It seemed like forever went by, and then I saw Charlie run across the yard. She crawled out through the small hole in the fence and joined me

---

* 1. Waiting gives you time to stress, worry and think. I thought about my soon-to-be cellmate Stab-a-Rasher.

2. Stab-a-Rasher was the name my dad gave to a murdering butcher in a ghost story he told us kids one Halloween when I was eight.

3. I woke up screaming that night. Dad didn't tell ghost stories after that, but the name stuck with me.

beyond the bushes, where I was waiting with the binoculars and our bikes.

'He did it,' she said. 'He pushed Titch into the van and the door closed behind him. It was cool.'

'So where is he?' He was supposed to get out of there and join us in the bushes.

'He'll be here – give him a minute,' she said.

I ignored her and looked through the binoculars. It was then I saw a number of vans leaving the warehouse and in the third van I saw my friend Sumo sitting up in the front seat, dressed as a security guard.

'Uh-oh,' I said.

'What?'

'Sumo's in the front seat of the van!'*

Charlie slapped her hand against her forehead, I threw on the backpack and then we were off and chasing them.

---

* 1. There was no plan that included Sumo sitting in the front seat of a security van.
 2. Sumo placed his hands on the glass and mouthed the word 'help' as he passed us.
 3. Big Tom's window was down and he was playing the Pogues singing 'Jesse James'. It's a song about a train robber, and it doesn't end well.

26

The Chase

We pedalled as quickly as we could to keep up with the van, but it was hard. Luckily, the roads were busy enough for it to have to slow down and stop a lot, giving us time to catch up whenever we fell behind. We bobbed and weaved through traffic. Charlie threw me the walkie-talkie, and as I put it in my pocket it crackled to life.

'Brown Bear, come in, Brown Bear.' It was Johnny J! But Sumo had been the last one to have the walkie-talkie. I was confused and beginning to regret using the handle Brown Bear.

'This is Brown Bear. You OK, Number One Buddy? Over,' I asked.

'I'm OK, but where's Cash? He threw in Titch

and the walkie-talkie and closed the door. Over.'

'He's in the front seat of the van. Over,' I said.

'WHAT?!' Johnny J said. He was so freaked out he forgot to say, 'Over.'

'Don't panic. We're on your tail. Do you have control of the van? Over?'

'Titch bit me, but we're fine. What are we going to do? Over.'

I didn't know what to do, and it was hard to think when I was trying to keep up with a van on a bike with a backpack full of Ireland gear and face paint on my back.

Suddenly Walker was on the walkie-talkie. 'Is he insane? What did he do that for? How are we going to come back from this?' He sounded frantic. Then he disappeared because the van got too far ahead for the signal to work. I had to speed up.

'Faster,' I shouted at Charlie. 'We need to go faster.'

She nodded and changed gears, I changed mine too and we sped up so much that our bikes wobbled. The walkie-talkie crackled back to life. Walker was still talking as though I'd been listening to everything he said.

'It's the only way. Agreed? Over,' he said.

'What's the only way? Over,' I said.

'I just said it. Over.'

'Well, I didn't hear it. Over.'

'Well, pay attention. Over.'

'I'm half killed trying to keep up with a speeding van. Over.'

'Oh, OK. Sorry. Over,' he said. 'We'll jump out with the bag of money after they make the first stop. Sumo'll have to make a run for it when he can. If he's sent into the bank, he'll just have to pretend to go inside and leg it, or if he's left in the van, he'll have to wait until Big Tom goes in and then leg it. Over.'

'OK. How will he know to do this? Over,' I asked.

'You'll have to stay behind and tell him. Over.'

Oh no. I thought. More pressure. My knees were buckling. I had not realised the first bank would be so far away. I also worried about the prospect of Sumo and Big Tom talking. What was Sumo saying? What were they talking about? I prayed it was football.

'OK. Over,' I said, and despite every muscle in my legs burning, I cycled on. Charlie kept up, but she was tired too.

'We'll be OK,' I called out to her.

178

'We have to be,' she said, and we cycled on for ANOTHER HOUR! AT BREAKNECK SPEED!

Eventually the van pulled in beside a large bank. As soon as I stopped, my legs gave way. I felt sick. Charlie flopped to the ground. Her bike fell on her. She didn't care.

'Water,' she gasped, but I didn't have any water. We watched Big Tom get out of the van and walk into the bank. This was my cue to run across and tell Sumo the new plan, but I couldn't stand up.

'Stand up,' Charlie said.

'I can't,' I said.

'Don't be so ridiculous.'

'You stand up then.'

She tried to stand up. She couldn't. 'Oh.'

I kneeled, then I climbed a little using my arms, holding on to a wall, and pulled myself up. Once I was on my feet I took one unsteady step, then another, and after a few seconds I was walking properly.

'Go,' she said as she pulled herself up using the wall.

My wobbly walk turned into a shaky run. I made it to the van and knocked on the window. Sumo rolled it down.

'Hi, Jeremy,' he said.

'What are you doing in the van?' I almost screamed.

'My best,' he said.

'The next time Big Tom goes into a bank, get out and run.'

'Any chance I could just run now?'

'The lads have to get the money and get out first,' I said.

He thought about it. 'OK. Do you know where we are?' he asked.

I hadn't got a clue. I moved to leave, but he stopped me.

'He's very nice,' he said, and I could tell he was feeling bad.*

'Sorry,' I said, and I don't know why I apologised except that I felt sorry.

'Me too.'

I shaky-ran back to Charlie, who was examining the blisters on her hand from gripping onto the handlebars. We got back on our bikes and waited for Big Tom to come out with the bag. It was a big bag and it looked full. He fed it through the slot on the side of the van and we saw it go in.

---

* 1. Tom had seven grandchildren.
  2. He was friendly.
  3. He shared Sumo's love of Spam.

'They have it,' I said. Then I radioed on the walkie-talkie, but we were parked too far away to communicate. I watched Big Tom get back in the van and the van take off.

'Let's go,' I said, and Charlie sighed deeply, closed her eyes, gripped the handlebars and took off. I followed, and we were giving chase once again.

'Number One Buddy, come in. Over. Tango, come in. Over?'

The walkie-talkie crackled to life.

'It's me, Tango. Number One Buddy is holding the bag. Over.'

'OK, great. Over.'

We followed the van until we reached a long queue of traffic and all the cars came to a standstill.

'I think there's been an accident up ahead,' Charlie said, and she cycled on to have a look.

'Tango, come in. Over?'

'Yeah? Over?'

'Looks like a traffic jam. Get ready to jump,' I said.

'Ready. Over.'

Charlie came back. 'Four cars – no one looks hurt, but the road's a mess,' she said. It was now or never.

181

'Jump out, turn left, into the shopping centre, meet in the toilets, over,' I said, thinking on the spot. Charlie nodded. I could see she was impressed.

The van door opened. Johnny J jumped out holding the bag and ran toward the shopping centre, but as Walker tried to follow, Titch broke free of his ropes and grabbed him. Walker dropped the pepper spray. Charlie and I watched from three cars back, frozen to the spot and really no help at all.

'Get off me,' Walker shouted.

'Hmm hummm hummmny hummmm,' Titch shouted, on account of the socks in his mouth. They pushed and pulled one another around the van. Titch pressed Walker's face up against the side of the van, but then when he tried to untie the scarf that held the socks in his mouth, he let go for a second and Walker made a run for it. As Walker ran out, Titch grabbed his jacket, but Walker was thin and wily and he escaped out of his own jacket. He'd got such a fright he ran right, not left as instructed. Just then Big Tom and Sumo jumped out of the van. Titch dropped the jacket and pulled the scarf off his face. He grabbed the can of pepper spray that Walker had dropped in the scuffle. Big Tom ran around to the back of the van in time for Titch to spray him in the face. Big Tom hit the ground moaning and crying, and poor Titch didn't know what to do. Then he saw us – Charlie and me. He looked right at us and pointed. My insides threatened to fall out, but before they did, he tripped over Walker's jacket and fell beside his moaning friend. Sumo had got such a shock he ran straight up the road toward the car crash.

Charlie and I looked at one another, frozen.

'Go,' I shouted, and we bolted on our bikes, weaving in and out of traffic, experts now, fire in our bellies as well as our legs. We were on the run with no idea where we were or where we were going. Only Johnny J and the bag were in the shopping-centre toilets. I tried to use the walkie-talkie, but of course it wasn't working.

'What now?' Charlie asked.

'The forest,' I shouted.

'How? Which way?' she shouted.

'I don't know!' I shouted back. We cycled on for a few minutes before we saw a 14A bus.

'It's a 14A!' Charlie shouted.

'Follow it,' I shouted back. She nodded and grinned. A 14A would guide us back to our area. It felt like a miracle.

27
The Panic

Charlie and I cycled till we reached the forest, where we promptly fell off our bikes and lay on the ground hugging our tired, screaming legs against our chests while moaning softly to ourselves. We did that for a long time. When we were done, we sat at the picnic table.

'Are you OK?' she asked.

'No,' I admitted.

'Good. Me neither.'

'Do you think they've been caught?' I asked.

'No,' she said.

'Good. Me neither.'

We were both lying, but it made me feel a bit better. The wait was torture, lunchtime became teatime and worry turned to abject fear. Suddenly all I could think was: *They've been caught, they've all been caught. We're going to get caught too.* I said it in my head over and over and then I saw him, large as life and waving at me from the distance. It was Sumo!

He sat down at the picnic table.

'I got the wrong bus. The traffic was terrible,' he said as though it was just a normal day and we hadn't robbed a cash van. Charlie asked him if he'd seen any of the others. He hadn't.

'How did you end up in the front seat of the van?' I asked.

'Oh, I pushed Titch into the back and Johnny J and Walker were waiting for him . . . That bit worked like a charm . . .' he said, and he took out a Spam sandwich and blew some pocket fluff off it before tucking in. We waited for him to finish. He was focused on the sandwich.

'And . . . ?' I said.

'Oh yeah, and as soon as the door was shut on Titch and the lads, Big Tom walked over, patted me on the back and asked me if I was filling in for Mr Brown. I didn't know what to say,' he said.

All of a sudden, Walker bobbed into view. 'I

heard the sirens so I hid for a while.' As we waited for Johnny J, Sumo explained that the van door was so heavy that it had shut itself after he pushed Titch in, and before he could reopen it, Big Tom had discovered him. 'I did my best,' he said, and we all agreed that he had. He was very stressed. He said that Big Tom had noticed how young he looked and asked him what cream he used or if he'd sold his soul.*

Sumo said he pretended to feel unwell to avoid answering questions. That's why Big Tom retrieved the money from the bank. 'He was being nice.'

Walker told us how Titch had fought Johnny J and bitten him hard and about how quiet he went when Walker threatened him. 'I scared myself,' Walker admitted.

He'd scared me too. My stomach ached. *What have we done? We're going to get caught. We're going to prison. WHAT HAVE WE DONE?*

Charlie talked about our hard cycle. The others didn't seem very impressed, even though our blisters and wobbly walks suggested we'd worked harder

---

* 1. 'Sold your soul' is a saying for when people are willing to do something bad for money or a favour or even a miracle.
   2. Big Tom didn't know it, but Sumo had sold his soul.
   3. We all had. *Gulp!*

than anyone else. Johnny J didn't arrive. At five o'clock we were dressing in our Ireland gear and painting our faces, but by then we feared the worst.

'He's definitely been caught,' Walker said.

'We're done for,' Sumo said.

'That idea to go into the toilets was stupid!' Walker said to me.

'Leave him alone,' Charlie shouted, and it was the first time Charlie Eastman stood up for me. It felt weird.

Then I remembered something – my brother Rich's stupid rehearsal for his stupid gig!

'What if he went straight to rehearsal?' I said.

'As if!' Walker said.

'No, listen, the rehearsal was at four. If he missed it, Rich would have tried to track him down, causing problems for all of us. If he was delayed like all of you were, he might have gone straight there.' I instantly felt better. I knew in my heart that if we went to the garage behind my house, we'd find Johnny J safe and well.

'It's going to be fine,' I said, wobbling onto my bike. 'Everything's going to be fine.'

Charlie and the boys followed me to my house. I could hear the music and Johnny J's voice singing before I saw him. A grin broke out on my face – never had Fingers & the Fudge sounded so good.

I opened the door and Johnny J grinned at me. I looked over to the bag of money that was casually lying on my parents' garage floor. The others pushed in behind me.

'What are you all doing here?' Rich said.

'We're your audience,' I said, and Buzz nodded.

'Cool,' he said. 'Sit down.'

'Nice gear,' Fingers said, pointing to us standing in our Ireland kit.

'Start again,' Rich said.

We all sat down on the ground, backs against the wall. The others watched our friend Johnny J sing and play his heart out with my brother Rich's crap band. I couldn't take my eyes off the bag of stolen money. There were so many things to worry about. Despite the flag painted on Sumo's face, Big Tom had spent enough time with him to identify him easily. Sumo said Big Tom had commented on the flag and liked his commitment to Ireland. I could tell that Sumo felt terrible about Big Tom by the fact that his head was hanging and he only ate half of his Spam sandwich. I'd never seen that before.

Then there was Walker to consider. Would Titch guess that Tango was actually his colleague's son? Titch hadn't said anything, but then it's hard to talk with balled socks in your mouth. And he'd seen Charlie and me cycle away. He looked at us with his beady little eyes, pointed at us with the sock still jammed in his mouth. What was he saying now that that sock was out? They'd know how many of us there were now for sure. Charlie's bike was pink. They'd know she was a girl. There we were, lined up against the wall in my parents' garage and dressed in Ireland gear, the same kids in gear the police were now looking for. We needed to change out of our disguises.

I waited till the rehearsal ended and Rich, Buzz, Cap and Johnny J high-fived. Fingers high-three'd on account of his three fingers.

'See you at Cornally's, Johnny J. Don't be late,' Rich said.

Johnny J nodded, picked up the black bag and swung it over his shoulders.

'What's in the bag?' Cap said. My heard raced, my palms sweated, ears buzzed. This was it, we were done for.

'Your mam,' Johnny J said, and all the lads laughed and high-fived/high-three'd again.

Johnny J didn't want to dress in the gear. He thought it was unnecessary, seeing the robbery was done and we didn't need to blend in any more, but Walker insisted we needed to be consistent – if we'd dressed up for the last match, why not this one? He had a point, plus I think he really liked it.

Johnny J was too tired to argue. I took the bag to the hiding spot in the forest while he changed and the others grabbed some food. I didn't look inside the bag, not when I was on my own. That bag of money scared me. It was heavy. I knew there was more than enough to send Mrs Tulsi to America. It should have made me feel better. It didn't. I felt the worst I've ever felt and I wanted to give it back.

Everyone agreed it was a better idea if we stayed apart till the match. It was seven o'clock. An hour to go. I lay on my bed. Downstairs, Mam was cleaning up after dinner, Dad and Rich were watching the build-up to the game. I couldn't. My heart wasn't in it. I heard the front door open and footsteps on the stairs and then my door opened and it was my sister Rachel.

I sat up.

'What are you doing here?' I asked.

'I came to see you,' she said, and she sat on my bed.

I shot up.

'Why?' I asked.

'I had a bad feeling,' she said, and I grew pale.

*A BAD FEELING!**

'What bad feeling?' I asked.

'Dunno,' she said. 'But you know even though I live across the city I'm always here for you, don't you, Jeremy?'

I said I did and then I cried in my sister's arms. I know, I know, I'm a big baby . . . But you'd cry too if you were a fugitive from the law with hand and butt blisters, wonky legs and a broken heart.

---

* 1. My brother said my sister was a witch, and not just because she was mean to him.

  2. She knew things, and I don't know how she knew them.

  3. Mr Lucey's black cat always sat on her bedroom windowsill and it even followed her onto the bus once. (Walker says that black cats love witches. Fact.)

28

The Match

Cornally's pub was packed to the rafters with what my dad described as every dog, duck and devil he'd ever met. To prove his point there were even a few dogs sleeping under tables. Sumo, Charlie and Walker sat together on the floor, eating free chips and staring up at the screen, lost in a game of football. Johnny J was engaged in some last-minute rehearsing behind the pub with Rich and the lads. I asked him if he was all right. He said he was and that it was good to have something to take his mind off everything.

I sat with my parents and Rachel. My mam was just delighted to have all her family together. I don't remember the first half of the Ireland v Netherlands match. I know Ireland was 1–0 down at half-time, but I was too busy thinking about everything that could still go wrong. Every time the door opened I worried it would be the guards coming in to drag us away, but as the time passed my fears eased.

Then it happened, just after seventy minutes of play. GOAL! GOAL! GOAL!* We were 1–1. Every dog, duck and devil jumped up and down and shouted, screamed, barked, cried and cheered. IRELAND, IRELAND, IRELAND! Johnny J, Rich and the lads started singing 'Jackie's Army' and everyone joined in. The match ended 1–1 and we were through to the knockouts. The Irish crowd in Cornally's pub, Dublin, watched the Irish crowd on a field in Palermo, Italy, singing and crying and the players jumping and high-fiving, and we all did the same.

Walker screamed that he'd seen his dad crying on the TV and then we all spotted him and he was bawling like a baby. 'He'll never live that down,' Walker said, and in that moment I forgot about

---

* 1. Packie Bonner drop-kicked a long ball, landing it in the Dutch 18-yard box.
  2. The Netherlands keeper Hans van Breukelen scrambled for it, but he spilled it in front of our advancing Niall Quinn.
  3. Niall Quinn slid and scooped the ball into the empty net!

Mrs Tulsi's illness, Auntie Alison's arrival, the robberies, the spectre of the guards arriving at our doorsteps, the prospect of prison, how disappointed and upset my parents would be if they knew what I had done. I forgot about everything and just celebrated with everyone else in the pub, and honestly it was probably one of the best moments of my life.

When the madness died down, some of the women with small babies and younger children left and I joined my friends at a table. Rich and the lads started setting up for the gig, but Johnny J came over to us instead.

'This is a sign,' Walker said. 'Everything's going to work out.'

'Deffo,' Charlie said.

'Between Ireland drawing 1–1 with the Netherlands and seeing that hummingbird – one hundred per cent,' I said.

Johnny J clapped his hands together. 'My mam is going to America. We've saved her. Thank you all. I mean it. Best friends ever,' he said, and he raised his glass of fizzy orange and we raised ours.

'Best friends ever,' we all shouted, and it was brilliant.

Everyone shushed when the post-match interview came on, but Rich wanted to get the gig going.

'Right, right, come on, Johnny J,' he said, coming over.

Johnny J smiled at me and gave me the thumbs up. I smiled, even though I was dreading the gig. Fingers & the Fudge were better with Johnny J, but they were still terrible.

Rich ushered Johnny J to the side of the small stage. (It looked more like a large box.) Buzz clapped him on the back. Fingers handed him his guitar.

'It's all set up,' he said, and Johnny J nodded. Cap pretended to be busy tapping and testing the microphone. He was clearly still annoyed that Johnny J was playing with them. When Rich turned on the actual speaker, Cap's voice came over loud and clear. 'Testing, one, two, three, testing.'

It was just then two policemen walked into the pub in full uniform. They looked serious, as though they were on a mission. This was it! This was the moment we'd be hauled off to jail. My fists clenched so hard I burst a few blisters. Sumo didn't notice them, but beside me Charlie and Walker's eyes were on sticks. Johnny J nearly dropped his guitar. The policemen looked around the pub, nodding at a few people. Then someone from the back started singing and the Garda joined in and Mr Cornally handed them both pints. We all sighed with relief. *Phew.* We were fine. Everything would be fine. Except it wouldn't.

29

The Gig

The post-match commentary went on till just after 10 p.m. The pub was still busy when the telly went off, and even before the band started playing, everyone was singing. Mr Cornally served out more chips. My mam had brought her own sliced pan and a pound of butter to make up chip sandwiches. Nobody really noticed the lads getting up on stage – they were eating chips, talking about the game, laughing, singing, hugging and crying happy tears.

Rich spoke to the crowd. 'Hello, Ireland,' he said, and no one paid attention. They were too busy having a good time to notice the kid on the stage. 'Hello, Dublin,' he roared again to the few people who bothered to listen.

Walker was patting his slightly swollen nose and making snorting sounds. 'I think I took an elbow to the face from Titch,' he said. 'I didn't feel it till now.'

'Yeah.' I nodded. 'Your nose is definitely bigger.'

'Nuts,' he said.

I looked over at Sumo. He was asleep in the corner. Charlie came and sat beside me. We didn't speak, not even one word. We were the only people in the room who had nothing to say. After a bit I looked her way. She smiled at me. I smiled back.

'It'll be OK,' she said, and that was that. We looked back onto the stage to Rich and the boys struggling to get attention.

'Would you all shut up and listen to these lovely boys?' my mam roared from the corner of the room. 'Go on, son,' she said, and everyone laughed and cheered.

Rich turned the colour purple, then he coughed a little and fixed his Lego-man hair before leaning into the mic.

'This is our first song. It's called "Take On Me", by A-ha,' Rich shouted, and stepped back from the mic. He clicked his fingers three times and then stepped back to the mic and started singing. On the second line of the song the rest of the boys joined in and Johnny J started to play, but the sound was too low.

'We can't hear ya,' someone roared.

'Eh? Hello?' Rich tapped the mic, 'Testing, one, two. Decko, will ya turn us up?'

Decko twiddled with loads of knobs.

'HELLLLLOOOOOOOO.' It was so loud the room shook!

'OK, TURN IT DOWN A BIT, DECKO.' The room rumbled with the sound of my brother's voice. My mam looked around the place anxiously. My dad dropped some chips out of his chip sandwich. Decko just pushed everything down again, so now Rich was just mouthing words. Some of the kids that went to school with us laughed and jeered. 'You're crap!'

Johnny J looked panicked, so I got up and went over to Decko.

'Hiya, Decko.'

'All right, Rich's brother?'

'Yeah, grand, thanks. Any chance you'd let me take over?'

199

'Ah yeah, great. I'm bursting for some chips,' he said, and he was gone.*

I took over. The sound wasn't perfect, but the lads could be heard. They were halfway into the first verse before the crowd really started to notice them. By the end of the second chorus they had them in the palm of their hands. Everyone was singing along, and every now and then someone would shout, 'Ooh aah Paul McGrath, ooh aah Paul McGrath.' By the time they sang U2's 'Bad', my dad was crying again.

'That's my son,' he said, pointing to the stage.

Johnny J sang really well and he was great on guitar, and for the first time I thought to myself, *This could be something.*

The boys left the stage to thunderous applause, and just like that they were local heroes. It was only when Johnny J got off the stage that I saw his Uncle Ted. He was waiting for him by the door. They hugged, a big bear hug. They held on to one another really tight. I think Uncle Ted was crying,

---

* 1. His job was to balance the sound.
  2. They might as well have asked our dead budgie (Ralph, spring 1986 to autumn 1987, RIP) to control the sound.
  3. Decko hadn't a clue.

200

but a lot of grown men cried that night, so no one took much notice.

Afterwards, Johnny J went missing. I looked for him and found him outside, sitting on the ground, leaning against the pub wall. I sat beside him.

'Good gig,' I said.

'Do you mean it?' he said.

'Yeah.' And I did. They were good. The crowd loved them.

'It was fun,' he said.

'I know.'

'What now?' he said. It was a good question.

'We buy your mam a ticket to New York City,' I said.

'But where in New York City?'

'The hospital.'

'What hospital?'

'I'm sure any of them will do,' I said.

'Do we even know where the hospital is?'

'No, but there's plenty of money for a taxi so . . .'

'Are we mad?' he asked.

'Yeah,' I said, 'but I told you before, my dad says everyone's mad.'

Uncle Ted came round from the back. 'You ready to go home?' he said.

'Yeah,' Johnny J said.

'I'll walk with you. I'll nip in to check on your mam and you can tell me all about this band.'

'Nothing to tell,' Johnny J said. 'It was just one gig.'

'Just one gig! No way – you have something there. Don't they, Jeremy?'

'Yeah.'

'You see,' Uncle Ted said, and he ruffled his nephew's hair. 'Rock stars.'

'What about Auntie Alison?' Johnny J said to his uncle, and Ted's smile faded and he held Johnny J by the shoulders.

'Don't you mind Auntie Alison,' he said, and Johnny J nodded and they hugged again. I just sat there.

'See ya tomorrow,' Johnny J said, and they started down the road. He spun around and walked backwards. 'And, Jeremy?'

'Yeah?' I said, struggling to get up off the ground.

'Best friends ever,' he said, and I grinned. He turned around and walked away.

I waited outside for my emotional father, my proud mother, my grown-up sister and my ultra-annoying brother to come out of the pub.

Rich was high on life. 'We are going to be the biggest band on the planet,' he said, punching the air.

'Ah you were fantastic, son, just fantastic, and, Jeremy, you were brilliant too. Wasn't he, Daddy?' my mam said.

'I did nothing,' I said.

'You twiddled those buttons. Didn't he, Ron?' Mam said, and Rachel grabbed my hand.

'Good job, Jeremy,' she said.

'Ace,' my dad said. 'Oh, it was some night. We'll remember this one, Debbie. It's one for the books all right.'

They talked and laughed and my dad chased my brother up and down the street before putting him in a headlock and ruffling his hair. Rich had tried to spike up his hair for the gig with gel. He looked like a Lego man who'd received an electric shock.

'Dad, Dad, me do! Don't mess with the hair.'

'Ah you're lovely, isn't he, Debbie? Isn't he lovely?'

My mam and Rachel just laughed.

Rich was busy protecting his hair. 'Ah no, seriously, it takes ages to do it.'

That night my mam and Rachel sat up drinking

tea and I could hear Rachel telling Mam about how lovely Rupert, her doctor boyfriend, was and how hard it was to be a nurse, and Mam told Rachel about how sad she was about her friend and how worried she was about Johnny J and me. I tried not to listen because I needed to sleep. There was still so much to do. What I didn't know as I drifted off was that a detective had Walker's jacket in his hand and that jacket had Walker's name written on the inside collar. It was only a matter of hours before they would connect Walker's jacket to Walker's dad, Walker's dad to Walker and Walker to the rest of us. Time was running out.

30

The Guards

For the first time in days I woke up feeling hungry.
I got dressed and made my way to the kitchen. I
was pouring cereal into a bowl when the phone
rang in the hall. My parents were moving around
upstairs. I think my mam was in the shower.

I walked into the hallway and picked up the phone.

'Hello, the Finn household. Who's speaking, please?'

'They're here. I mean not here – they're at my
house.' It was Walker.

'Are you joking?' I asked. I knew he wasn't. I
just had to be sure. He wasn't joking.*

---

* 1. He had jumped from his sister's second-storey bedroom window and
landed on an old trampoline they had in the garden.
2. He was calling me from a phone box down the street from his house.
3. There was no going back now.

'Are you OK?' I stammered.

He didn't bother answering. Instead we agreed he'd pick Charlie up and go to our spot in the forest.

'What will I say to Mrs Eastman?'

'Make something up.'

'OK, what about you?'

'I'll ring Sumo and grab Johnny J. We'll meet you there.'

'OK, and get Sumo to bring the rest of the money,' he said.

'Why?'

'Because we're going to need it.'

'What do you mean?'

'I mean we're on the run now, Jeremy,' he said, and it's a miracle I didn't faint because I actually heard my brain pop.

Walker hung up. I sat on the hall stairs with my head in my hands. *How am I going to tell Johnny J?*

My dad came down the stairs.

'Who was that?' he asked.

'No one.'

'Well, it must have been someone.'

'It was a wrong number,' I said.

'Not someone looking for that vet's two streets over again?'

'Yeah.'

'Oh, I am so sick of people ringing the wrong number. Since when has 845612 been 845912? Six and nine are two different numbers. How hard it is to get it right?' He was so busy ranting he didn't even notice me dialling Sumo's number. 'That's the trouble with people – they don't know how to dial a phone, and who'd be calling a vet so early in the morning anyway?' he said before closing the kitchen door behind him. *Someone with a sick animal,* I thought. I didn't say it. I was too frantic to be cheeky.

Mrs Lane answered the phone.

'This is the Lane household, who's calling, please?' she said.

'Hiya, Mrs Lane, it's Jeremy. Is Sumo around?'

'He's eating his breakfast, Jeremy.'

'Any chance I could have a word? It's just for a project in school.'

'They're giving you projects? During the summer holidays?' she said.

'Only if we want to,' I said. 'We really like learning,' I lied.

'Good for you, love. I'll get him.'

I could hear her shouting Sumo's name and then I waited for what seemed like forever. *Come on, come on.*

I knew that as Walker and Charlie were running to the park and I was making calls, Walker's mother would be answering the guard's questions. *Who does Walker hang out with?* Sumo would be top of the list. There was no time to waste.

'I didn't know we had a project!' Sumo said, and he sounded really stressed.

'We don't. The guards are at Walker's.'

'Oh,' Sumo said. 'That's much worse than a project.'

'You need to get to the forest.'

'For what?'

'I dunno, Sumo. We need a plan.'

'OK.'

'Leave now.'

'OK.'

'Don't tell your parents where you're going.'

'OK.'

'Bring a bag and the money from the fights and Rolands'.'

'OK.'

'And sandwiches – you're going to need lots of Spam sandwiches.'

'OK. Jeremy?'

'Yeah.'

'Are we going to jail now?'

'Probably,' I said.

'Right then.'

Sumo hung up the phone. My dad was still talking to himself in the kitchen. 'Six is not nine. Nine is not six.' Mam was moving around upstairs and singing 'Eye of the Tiger' to herself. Rich was still sound asleep on his bed, probably dreaming about being a rock star. I forgot Rachel was home.

I ran upstairs and filled my backpack with some underwear, my toothbrush, a comb, jeans and two jumpers. I grabbed my jacket and left the house as quietly as I could. As I turned away from the door, I saw Rachel sitting on our front wall. She instantly saw the backpack.

'What's that?'

'Nothing.'

'It's something.'

'I'm doing a school project,' I said, and Rachel laughed. She wasn't as easily fooled as Mrs Lane.

'A school project during the summer before you go to an entirely different school?'

'It's voluntary,' I said.

'What are you up to, Jeremy?' she said, and I wanted to confess everything but I couldn't. We had to get Johnny J's mother to America.

'How come you are sitting out here?' I said, turning the tables on her.

'Just thinking.'

'And smoking,' I said.

'I'm eighteen. I can do what I want,' she said. She was right. She could, except that my mam would kill her stone dead if she found her smoking.

'Smoking is stupid,' I said, and she nodded.

'I know.'

'So why do you do it?' I asked.

She shrugged.

'Mrs Tulsi has cancer. Smoking causes cancer,' I said, and Rachel sighed.

'I know.'

'You're a nurse.'

'OK, Jeremy, I know. It's stupid. I'm stupid. You've made your point. So just go,' she said, and I ran to Johnny J's and I didn't look back even once.

Johnny J answered the door.

'What's going on?'

'Get your coat,' I said.

'It's warm outside.'

'Yeah, well, it might be cold tomorrow. Pack some stuff.'

He gave me a really funny look. 'What?'

'We need to go, Johnny J,' I said. 'We need to go now.'

'Why?'

'The police were at Walker's first thing this morning.'

'You're messing.'

'Wouldn't about this.'

'Right,' he said. He looked around and up the stairs. 'What about Mam?'

'We'll work it out.'

'I need to say goodbye.'

'We don't have time,' I pleaded.

'I have to.'

He ran up the stairs. I stood there looking around, waiting for the police car to make its way down the road, and then I saw it snake toward me. I jumped inside Johnny J's house, and without even thinking, I ran up his stairs, two steps at a time.

'Johnny J,' I whispered urgently. I crept over to where his mam's room was. Through the crack in the door I could hear him talking to her.

'I'm just going out, Mam. I won't be long. There's your water. Do you see it? On the locker.'

'I see it, son.'

'Auntie Alison will be here soon and Uncle Ted after work.'

'She's moved into that fancy hotel,' she said, and she laughed to herself. 'She couldn't stick it here. I had afternoon tea in that hotel once with your daddy. Fifteen quid for a few triangle sandwiches with no crusts and a cup of tea!'

'Will you eat something for me, Mam?' he said.

No time, no time, they're here, I shouted in my head.

'No, son, you go.'

Yes, son, go, go, go!

'I love you, Mam.'

'I love you too, son. Don't worry about me, OK?' she said.

'OK.'

He walked into the hall and he closed his mother's door behind him. I was standing in front of him when the doorbell rang.

'They're here,' I whispered and his face changed colour. He ran to the front window and we could see two men standing at the door. Both wore coats, and suits under their coats, and they had their IDs in their hand.

'It's over,' Johnny J said, and his eyes threatened to fill and his lip trembled.

'It's not over,' I said, looking down at the tops of the two men's heads. 'We need to go –' held out my hand – 'NOW.'

He nodded, and as the police were knocking on the front door we were running for the back door.

31

The Money

Johnny J's house was terraced. It didn't have an entrance on one side like ours. His garden backed on to an elderly woman's. She was called Mrs Shanley.* We scrambled over the wall and I could hear Mrs Shanley playing her piano as we made our way into her garden. I got caught in her roses. They tore chunks out of my legs and arms. Johnny J pulled me out, but not before I'd trampled her pink ones. Two of the cats were sitting in the garden just staring at us. One hissed as we passed.

---

* 1. Mrs Shanley was a piano and guitar teacher who gave Johnny J free
   lessons.
2. She had ten cats. Nine were alive and one was stuffed, with beads for
   eyes, and she kept it on her windowsill.
3. She was English, but to escape the bombings she came to Ireland as a
   child during World War Two.

'What are we going to do now?' I said, and I was panicked. The only escape was through Mrs Shanley's house. Johnny J checked her back door. It was locked.

Johnny J knocked at the door.

'What are you doing?' I whisper-shouted.

'Getting us out of this,' he said.

Mrs Shanley came to the door.

'Hello?' she called. 'Who's there?'

'It's me, Johnny J!' he said, and she opened the door and smiled.

'Ah, love, I wasn't expecting you today.'

'Hiya, Mrs Shanley. I'm not here for a lesson and sorry to bother you, but would it be all right if we came through your house?' Johnny J said.

'Who's this?' she said, looking at me.

'My friend Jeremy,' he said, and that's when Mrs Shanley moved over and took my face in her hands and took a good look at me.

'Oh,' I said. It was a shock to be touched by old hands. They looked like melted ice-cream on a hot day. I felt faint.

'A lovely boy,' she said before pulling gently on my ponytail. 'I like the hair.'

Johnny J laughed a little. He really liked Mrs

Shanley. There was a cat at the top of the stairs, a cat at the bottom and two in the kitchen, but the house was sparkling clean and smelled of lemon not cats.

'Do you like cats?' she asked me.

I nodded yes.

'Always keep a cat – they'll let you know when a bomb is about to drop.'

'OK,' I said.

'Their fur rises, and if they run, you run,' she said.

'OK,' I said again.

'So why do you need to go through my house?' she asked as we walked through her kitchen. It was then the police sirens started to peal out.

Mrs Shanley listened to them and looked at us. She stood between us and the front door and freedom. One of the cats on the stairs darted onto the landing, her fur standing on end. That was not a good sign, and Mrs Shanley knew it.

'We really have to go,' Johnny J said, and I thought, *That's it, we're finished*, but Mrs Shanley nodded her head slowly as she thought about things.

'Go on,' she said, opening her front door and letting us out.

'Mrs Shanley, will you tell my mam and my Uncle Ted I'm sorry,' Johnny J said when we were outside.

'What trouble have you got yourself into, pet?' she asked as the sirens grew closer.

'Did you know that they can cure cancer in America, Mrs Shanley,' he said.

'Oh, love,' she said, and tears sprang in her eyes. 'Please stay. Whatever you've done, we'll work everything out.'

'I can't. Not yet. Tell them, Mrs Shanley, won't you?' he said, and the sirens sounded so close we started running and we didn't stop until we arrived at our spot in the forest.

Charlie was there, hanging upside down from a tree, her eyes red from crying. Sumo had the large bag of money between his legs. Walker was walking around in circles.

'About time,' he said.

'They were at Johnny J's,' I said.

'That means they know about us all,' Charlie said as she jumped down off the tree. We sat around the picnic table. I could picture them in my house, telling tales and upsetting my parents' morning. If Rich was awake he was probably loving this, although now that Johnny J was in his band maybe he'd be concerned. Either way, we were in very big trouble.

'But how?' I asked. 'How could they know it was us?'

Walker put up his hand. 'It was me,' he said, and no one understood what he was talking about. 'I overheard them telling my mam. My jacket – Titch grabbed it off me. My name was stitched into the lining.'

'Oh, Walker!' I said.

'Sorry,' he said. 'I didn't think.' I could see that he felt terrible. There was no point in saying anything to him. Every kid in the country had their name sewn into clothes back then. It was just something mothers did.

'What now?' Sumo said.

Walker got up and walked around in circles again before shaking his head wearily and looking to me.

'We save Mrs Tulsi,' I said.

'We need to buy that plane ticket,' Johnny J said.

'And then what?' Charlie said.

'We post the ticket and some cash to Mrs Tulsi and we go on the run,' I said.

'For how long?'

'How long does the post take?' I said.

Walker thought about it and sniffed and held his swollen nose. 'Two days.'

'Look, the important thing is we get Mrs Tulsi on a plane, so we buy the ticket, post it and stay hidden until she is in America,' I said, and everyone agreed.

'What then?' Charlie asked.

'I don't know,' I said.

Everyone grew very quiet. We were all scared and sad and sick. It was a terrible moment. It was time to open the bag of money and count out the amount we needed for the ticket. Sumo lifted the bag onto the picnic table and unzipped it, and as soon as he touched the stacks of cash, there was a massive purple explosion. We all ducked, except for Sumo. He turned to me with a purple face and blinking eyes.

'What happened?' he asked, looking at his purple hand.

'You're purple,' I said. Then I looked at the money. 'The money is purple too.'

We all looked from a purple Sumo to a pale Walker.

219

'Did you know about this?' Charlie asked. 'What is this stuff?'

'They're dye packs,' said Walker.

We all looked at him as if he was talking a different language.

'They're set to explode if the money is robbed,' he explained.

'Well, why didn't you mention it?' I almost screamed.

'I've seen it on the TV! I didn't actually think they were used in real life!' he said.

'This comes off, right?' Sumo said, rubbing his hand.

'No, don't touch it!' Walker said. 'The whole point is that it stains.'

'Oh no,' Sumo said.

Johnny J didn't care if it stained him. He opened the bag up and shook all the money out on the picnic table, looking for enough unstained notes to buy his mam a ticket to America. He was frantic, until eventually he found a stack that was untouched by the dye.

'One thousand and five pounds,' he said, and he held it close to his chest. 'With the other money, it's plenty.' We took the unstained cash and left the rest – it was no good to us and just weighed us down. Although we had the money we needed, we also now had a large purple-faced Sumo that would give us away to law enforcement.

'What do we do about Sumo?' I asked.

Charlie took her pink scarf off. 'Put this on,' she said, and Sumo wrapped it around his face, only leaving room for his eyes.

'It looks too obvious,' I said.

'It's better than purple dye,' she said.

I disagreed, but we didn't have time for an argument. It wouldn't be long before the police started combing the forest for us. We needed to go.

'We'll get a mask for him in town. Now it's time to go,' Charlie said, and we were on the move once more.

32

The Ticket

We took the bus into town. We sat at the back on the top deck. It was a Friday. There were no World Cup games on that day, but the city was still decked out in green, white and gold and everyone who passed us seemed to have an extra pep in their step, strangers saying 'Howya' to one another and everyone smiling, laughing, upbeat. The sun was still shining and it felt like the only people with troubles in Dublin, Ireland, that day were us and our families. Every time I thought about my family I wanted to cry. They had been so happy the night before. I had ruined that now. *Sorry, Mam and Dad. Sorry, Rachel. Sorry, Rich.*

We got off the bus on O'Connell Street. There

was a travel agent on the corner of Talbot Street. Charlie went off in search of a mask, Sumo hid in a doorway and Johnny J and I went inside while Walker watched for police. The bell rang out as the door opened and a blonde lady in a red suit and white silk scarf looked up from her computer and smiled at us.

'How can I help?'

'We'd like to buy a ticket for New York, please,' Johnny J said, and she looked us up and down and pointed.

'You'd like a ticket for New York?'

Johnny J nodded. 'It's for my mam.'

'Oh, and she sent you to buy it?' she said.

'She's not well.'

'Oh, I'm sorry,' she said. 'Sit down.' She pointed to some chairs in front of a desk.

We sat down. I put my backpack, which held the money, under the chair and between my legs.

'When would she like to travel?' she said.

Johnny J and I looked at one another. *Good question.*

'As soon as possible,' I said, and Johnny J nodded furiously.

'Yeah, ASAP.'

'OK,' she said, 'well, it will take about a week for the ticket to be processed and sent out, so I'll book for fourteen days from now.'*

How were we going to outsmart the law for two whole weeks? Johnny J looked like he was about to throw up.

'I was hoping for sooner,' he said, and the lady laughed.

'We're not magicians,' she said.

'It's fine,' I said.

'The ticket costs seven hundred and eighty pounds,' she said.

'Grand,' I said. I opened my bag and counted out the money.

When I handed her the exact amount, she looked from us to the cash and I held my breath. Then she smiled and nodded. 'Right then.'

She asked us loads of questions about Johnny J's mam, including her middle name, the details of her address and phone number, and then he answered questions about what meal she'd like and where she'd like to sit on the plane. He said she'd

---

* 1. Before everyone had computers, people had to buy plane tickets from travel agents.
2. You had to book way in advance.
3. The tickets were posted out to your home.

have the chicken and asked if they'd seat her beside the toilet if possible.

'So you'll have those tickets out to her ASAP,' he said as we were leaving.

'Yes, sir,' she said.

'Thanks,' he said.

'Just before you go – does she have a visa?' she asked.

'A visa?' Johnny J looked from the travel agent to me.

'Yes, a visa to get her into America?'

'I don't think so. Does she need a visa?'

'Oh yes.'

'Well, how does she get one?' Johnny J sounded very upset.

'She'll have to go to the American Embassy.' She riffled through a drawer and handed us a lot of forms. 'She'll need to fill out forms like these.'

'In the embassy?' Johnny J asked.

I pushed forward. 'And then she can go to America?'

'Unless she has a criminal record,' she said, and she smiled.

'No, she doesn't,' Johnny J said.

'Good, shouldn't be a problem then.'

We met up and all headed to a doughnut shop

on O'Connell Street and sat around a table eating doughnuts bought with the proceeds of crime and working out our next move. We all agreed that the only thing we could do was post a letter to Mrs Tulsi telling her to get an American visa and to expect a ticket to turn up within ten days.

'Of course, that makes her an accomplice to our crimes,' Walker said.

'Well, being an accomplice is better than being dead,' Johnny J said. He was right.

We finished up our doughnuts and headed to the General Post Office and congregated in a corner of the giant room. Johnny J wrote a letter to his mam and Uncle Ted on the back of an old brown paper bag that someone had left in the wastebasket.

Dear Mam and Uncle Ted,

There's a ticket on the way to you for America. Please use it. Here's money for expenses. Please get on the flight and get a taxi and go to the hospital – ask the taxi man which hospital is the best one for you. Walker says that taxi men know everything. They will fix you, Mam. I'm sorry that we couldn't get enough money to send Uncle Ted with you and I'm sorry I've had to go away. Please tell the Finns, Browns, Lanes and Eastmans that we are all OK and that we are very sorry for everything.

I'll miss you, Mam, but I'll see you again.
USE THAT TICKET.
Big love,
Johnny J.

PS Uncle Ted, please check Mam's passport is up to date and take her to the American Embassy to get a visa. It's very important.
Thanks, Johnny J.

I handed him most of the money we had left, only keeping one hundred pounds for us. I figured one hundred pounds would do the five of us for as long as we needed it. He put the money and letter into a big envelope, sealed it and posted it.

'What now?' he said.

'Now we hide,' I said.

'Where?' Charlie said, and we all just stood there in the middle of the General Post Office, not having a clue where to go.

'The zoo?' Sumo said. We all looked at him, hiding behind the pink scarf. He just shrugged. 'I just like the zoo,' he mumbled.

'Maybe hide out in the Dublin Mountains?' Charlie suggested.

'What if it rains?' I asked.

'I'll die out on a mountain,' Walker said, and then took a blast of his inhaler just to make his point.

After what seemed like a really long time, Sumo put his purple hand up in the air. 'My Auntie Nora has a caravan in Wexford.'

'Any chance she'd be there?' I said.

'Nah,' he said. 'She hates Wexford.'

'Do you know how to get there?'

He hunched. 'Mam and I got the train down a few times. The place is called Strawberry Beach Park.'

'That'll do,' I said, and we walked outside onto the street. I saw a taxi coming up the road and I put my hand out.

'Taxi,' I shouted.

The guy stopped.

'Will you take five of us?' I said.

'I'll take ten of you if you're paying,' he said.

We all piled in.

'Where to?' he said.

'Heuston Train Station,' I answered, and that was it. Johnny J, Sumo, Walker, Charlie and I were officially on the run.

33
The Train

In the summer of 1990, trains were not as they are today. They were slower. The engine was a lot louder. The carriages were attached to one another by something that looked like a bockety old rubberised concertina. The seams between the carriages shook and shuddered and felt really unsafe. I always jumped over them. Charlie seemed to like them though. She stood right on the dodgy join with her arms spread wide and her fingers touching each side of the rubberised wall. She closed her eyes and just shuddered and shook for the longest time.

Sumo, Walker, Johnny J and I sat opposite one another in two two-seaters with a table between us. It was like the picnic table in our forest, except the seats had backs and instead of timber slates they were solid and the fabric was so rough that it felt like they had been upholstered in carpet. The table had cigarette burns in it, but other than that it was covered in crisps, chocolate and really dry sandwiches we'd bought from the cart.*

The carriage was busy but not full. Four girls in their twenties sat opposite us. Even though it was early in the day, they were drinking and singing songs about love. One of the girls was wearing a veil and a set of L-plates. They were louder than the really loud train engine. They tried to talk to us.

'Where you off to, boys?' the girl with the veil said.

'Nowhere,' Walker said.

'Oh yeah, where's that then?' she said.

'It's just past none of your business,' he said,

---

* 1. In the 1990s, people smoked on pretty much all forms of transport, including trains and planes, and in cinemas, restaurants, pubs, clubs and even in hospitals. The smell was gross.

2. Ireland's most popular sandwich was dry bread, thick butter and a thin slice of ham. Also gross.

3. Carpet-upholstered seats can cause a rash. I don't want to say where, but I think you know. Really, really gross.

and I was worried he was being a bit rude, but the girls laughed.[*]

'Hey, Scarf-face?' another girl said, and she was talking to Sumo. 'What age are you?' She had so much black eye make-up on that at first glance you could be forgiven for thinking a panda had escaped from the zoo.

Sumo froze.

'Thirty-five,' Walker said.

'Is he the only one with a mouth?' she said, and the rest of us just stared at her, scared to say a word. Although we were criminals, we weren't as confident or as rude as Walker.

'We'll get a taxi to Strawberry Beach Park,' I whispered to the others.

'Do they have taxis in Wexford town?' Johnny J said.

It was a good question. I didn't know. 'There will definitely be a bus?' I said, but everyone could tell I wasn't sure.

'Ah have you ever been to Wexford?' Walker said. 'It's a country kip.'

---

[*] 1. Walker was the rudest and most sarcastic person I knew.
   2. Older people mostly seemed to find him really endearing and funny.
   3. Johnny J said that was because he was small and he had big hair.

'No, it's not, it's lovely,' Sumo said.

'So why does your auntie hate it then?'

'Because my mam says she has a cold soul,' he said.

'How far is it from the train station?' I asked.

'Dunno,' he said. 'I wasn't paying attention.'

Charlie returned to the table and grabbed a sandwich. Johnny J tried to make room for her by pushing me into the window. She sat on the arm of his seat.

'I've been thinking – we just have to keep our heads down for two weeks, time for Johnny J's mam to get a visa to America and for that ticket to come in the post. As soon as she's gone we can hand ourselves in –'

'Hand ourselves in?' Walker said.

'Well, what do you think we're going to do, genius?' she said, and Walker was stumped.

'Exactly,' she said. 'In the meantime, I don't know about you, but I've never been to the beach, so let's make this a holiday, the best holiday ever.'

'Because after we hand ourselves in we're going to be locked up?' Walker said.

'Probably,' she said, 'but if Johnny J's mam survives it will be worth it.' She looked around at us. 'Won't it, Jeremy? I mean, that's what you've been thinking all along, isn't it?' she said.

'I suppose so,' I said, and for some reason I cheered up a little. 'No matter what happens to us, it'll be worth it.'

Sumo nodded and slapped the table. 'Totally worth it.'

Walker sighed. 'Yeah, absolutely, of course,' he said. 'Of course, we'll probably die because our mams will murder us before we ever get to jail.'

We all nodded. 'Yeah.'

Johnny J grinned at us and he looked like he might cry, but he didn't. I wished I could be more grown-up like Johnny J. 'Best friends ever,' he said, and beamed at all of us.

'That's it then,' Charlie said. 'We're going on holiday.'

Suddenly I felt a weight lifting. I didn't have to pretend that we weren't going to get caught any more, because we were! Now all we had to do was have two weeks of the best fun ever, and after that? Well, I didn't want to think about after that and neither did anyone else. We spent the rest of the train journey playing games of I spy and laughing at jokes, and we even joined in when the girls opposite sang Madonna's 'Holiday' for the fifth time in an hour.

34

The Town

We stepped off the train in Wexford and we may as well have been in a foreign country. It's hard to describe how, but it was just so different from Dublin. It was even warmer for a start! I was sweating buckets before we left the station. The town was weird; the shops were all different colours and one of them had a straw roof. There were two horses just randomly tied to lamp posts, eating feed from bags. There was a man and a donkey walking down the centre of the road, and instead of beeping him all the cars just went around him. The strangest thing of all was everyone waved at each other and said hello and stopped to talk about the weather and how good it was. The accents were odd – some of them I couldn't even understand. The only thing that felt familiar was the green, white and gold bunting that hung around the lamp posts and fluttered above the town.

Sumo stopped dead at a shop that had buckets and spades outside and a picture of ice-cream cones in the window. He turned to us. 'These are the best ice-cream cones ever,' he said before putting out his hand. 'Money me.'

I took out a fiver and handed it to him.

'You won't be sorry,' he said.

He came out minutes later with five large cones with chocolate flakes sticking out of them. He handed them out. Sumo was wrong about many things, but he was not wrong about those cones. They were and still are the best ice-cream cones I'd ever tasted.

We walked around, soaking the place up. Strangers said hello and we said, 'Hiya,' back to them. It was nice. It was new and exotic and weird and even a bit cool. It was scary too. We didn't know if the people of Wexford were aware that five kids from Dublin were fugitives on the run. Maybe our photo was in every police station in Ireland by now. We might even be in the national newspapers or on the telly!!!

236

At one point we saw a police car. Walker yelped and ran into a shop. Johnny J grabbed Charlie and they ducked behind a car. I turned my back to the car and pretended I was looking in a clothes-shop window. Sumo just stood in the middle of the street, frozen to the spot, his face covered in a pink silk scarf. The police car passed and disappeared. We all turned to Sumo.

'You've got to stop freezing, Sumo!' Walker said.

'Sorry,' Sumo said.

Charlie went into a comic shop, and when she came out, she handed Sumo a Star Wars Wookie mask. 'Put that on,' she said.

'Cool,' Sumo said. 'This is even better than Vader.' He put it on and gave her back her scarf. 'Better?' he asked.

'Much better,' I said.

'It suits you,' Charlie said, and she was right, it did.

We walked around for a while. We couldn't see a taxi rank and we weren't sure where the bus station was, so Walker appointed Sumo our Wexford Liaison Officer and/or Guide (which meant he was to do all the talking).

Sumo approached a youngish fellow sitting on

a tractor, drinking out of a flask and smoking a cigarette. He had a trailer half filled with straw attached. A three-legged dog was asleep on one of the wrapped bales.

'Hiya, can you tell us how long it would take to walk to Strawberry Beach?' Sumo said.

'Well, Wookie, that depends. How quick are you on your feet?' the fellow asked.

'Quick enough.'

'Yeah, but on a scale of one to ten? One being "walking on broken legs slow" and ten being "Stephen Roche on a bike fast"?'*

Sumo thought about it. 'I'd say we're about a solid five,' he said.

The guy took a long drag from his cigarette. 'Well then, I'd say you'd be walking for about forty-five minutes.'

'Which way?' Sumo said.

The guy pointed. 'That way.'

'Is it a straight run?'

'If crooked is straight.'

'No, it's not.' Sumo was muddled.

---

* 1. Stephen Roche was a famous Irish cyclist.
2. He won the Tour de France, the Giro d'Italia and the World Road Race Championship.
3. He was considered the fastest man in Ireland.

'Correct, there's more twists and turns than a Stephen King novel.'

'Right,' Sumo said. 'Thanks.'

He turned to us. 'He's very hard to talk to.'

The guy laughed. 'I'm just playing with you. Forgive me, kiddo, it's the Wexford way. Get on the trailer.'

I pointed to myself and said, 'All of us?'

'Go on. I'm passing that way.'

We jumped aboard and soon we were travelling down the twisting, turning roads of Wexford, blinking at the blue sky, the sun beating down, a three-legged dog panting at us and our stomachs full of ice cream. I missed my mam and dad, Rachel and even Rich. I was worried about going to prison and knew life would never be quite the same again, but right then and there, I was having fun.

He pulled up at an old wooden sign with red strawberries on it, but it was missing its *S* and *Y*, so it read 'trawberr Beach Park'.

'Betty Bloomers will take care of you,' he said as we got off the trailer and thanked him.

'Who's Betty Bloomers?' I asked, just as a woman came out, with a head full of black curls and a short patterned dress and what looked like long knickers with frills peeping from just under the dress.

'She's Betty Bloomers,' Sumo said.

'What can I do for you?'

'I'd like to stay in my aunt's caravan.'

'Does she know you're coming?'

'It's a surprise,' he stammered.

'Who's your aunt?'

Sumo gave the name, and also mentioned his uncle who'd died and their dog who was still alive, as far as he knew.

'I'm really sorry, but your aunt sold the caravan.'

'When?'

'Last spring.'

'Oh.'

'Can you rent us another caravan?' Johnny J asked.

'I'm sorry, we're full.'

'Any other parks around here that we can try?' Johnny J said.

She thought about it for a moment. 'Is it just you five?' she said.

'Yeah.'

'Where are your parents?'

'At home.'

'And they let you come to Wexford alone?'

240

'We're older than we look,' Charlie said.

The woman said, 'Hmmmmmmmmmmm.' She was staring at Sumo in his Wookie mask. She didn't look convinced. 'Business is booming down here. With the matches and all, half the country has taken holidays, but I know a man who has a caravan on his land. It's doing nothing, so maybe he'll let you stay.'

'We have money,' I said.

'Well, I hope so – he's as miserable as sin, this fella. Give me a minute.' She went inside to make a telephone call.

We sat down on the ground and waited.

'Do you think she's calling the police?' Charlie said.

'I don't know, but get ready to run.' We waited nervously, all ready to run for the hills if we noticed anything out of place.

Betty Bloomers came out after a few minutes. 'He'll give it to you for one pound a day if you milk his cows, feed the hens and help him fix one of the fences.'

No one had been expecting that. We just stared at her blankly, waiting for her to say that she was joking.

'It sleeps six,' she said.

'OK,' Johnny J said.

'Good. I'll tell him,' she said. 'Oh, and he said he'd feed you, but only if you do the cooking.'

'None of us can cook,' I said.

'I can make scrambled eggs and ham-and-mushroom omelettes,' Charlie said.

'I can make vegetable soup and spaghetti bolognese,' Johnny J said. I did not know that about him.

'Great,' she said. 'It's a deal.' She took a pen and paper out of her pocket. 'Now, the farm is called Jimbo's and there's a scarecrow at the gate,' she said as she scribbled on the page. 'Here are the directions.' She handed me the page. 'If you get lost, look for smoke – he lights a turf fire even on a hot day.'

We thanked her and moved to leave.

'And whatever you do, don't make him angry.'

'Why?' Sumo said. 'What happens?'

'Well, you wouldn't like him when he's angry,' she said in a tone of voice that suggested she was foreshadowing evil.

'How do you know?' Sumo said, and he sounded scared.

'He's my daddy,' she said brightly, and she winked and went inside.

So we had a choice: become slaves to a mean and angry man, or sleep outside.

'He can't be that bad,' Walker said, and he started walking toward the old man, the smoke and the scarecrow.

35
The Farm

We followed the smoke, and as we had to climb stone walls and jump over fences, avoid a large angry bull and run through some very skittish sheep, I'm guessing we managed to find the long and awkward way to Jimbo's farm. We walked past the scarecrow, up the winding narrow path and, standing in his doorway, there was Jimbo, the oldest, gnarliest and scariest man I'd ever seen. He looked like a killer from a horror comic and I genuinely wanted to run. *Oh no, this is where we get caged, fattened, cooked and eaten. Goodbye, Mam and Dad. Goodbye, Rachel. See ya, Rich. I suppose we had it coming!*

The old man standing in his darkened doorway

was so thin he looked like a skeleton with a face. He had a white beard that reached his chest and he wore a red bandana on his bald head. His fingers were so long it reminded me of the alien from the movie *E.T.* When he talked, his voice sounded like sandpaper, and his eyes were so watery that it looked like he was crying even though he wasn't. It took a few minutes of him talking at us before I realised he was blind. He totally and completely freaked me out, and I'm not proud of this, but I did step behind Charlie, who didn't seem to mind the man at all.

'My daughter says you'll do some work for me.'

'Yes, sir,' Johnny J said.

'Jimbo is my name-o,' Jimbo said.

'OK, Jimbo,' Johnny J said. It was the first time an adult had ever told one of us to call them by their first name.

'What's your name?'

'Am, ah, aaahhh . . .' We hadn't thought about fake identities, but we definitely needed them.

'He's Alvin,' I said, stepping out from behind Charlie, and out of habit I pointed to Johnny J. Then I pointed to Walker. 'He's Simon,' I said, looking at Walker, who was cleaning his spectacles

245

and then I pointed to Sumo in his Wookie mask. 'And that's Theo. I'm Dave.'

'I'm Brittany,' Charlie said, and I sighed with relief. She got it.*

'You kids have some weird names,' Jimbo said.

'Thanks,' I said.

'Right, bring me to the caravan,' he said, and he picked up the white stick that was leaning on the wall. 'Head for the smell of cow dung.' He reached out and I was the closest to him, so he grabbed on to my arm with his alien fingers. My stomach felt sick. *Oh no. Be cool, Jeremy. Just be cool.*

The smell of dung was unholy (my mam's friend Laura used to call anything really bad 'unholy', and that dung was UNHOLY) and the caravan looked like a really large metal bin. It was rusted and resting on bricks. Some of the bricks were broken or missing, so it slanted toward the back end. Jimbo felt for the door and pulled it open and a small bird flew out, along with a smell like petrol, burnt toast, a little bit of poo and a lot of wee and lavender.

---

* 1. The names came from the TV show *Alvin and the Chipmunks*.

2. I loved that show.

3. I knew the theme song off by heart and sang it in my head when I got nervous. I'd been singing it in my head a lot lately.

'There you go, boys – home sweet home,' he said. 'Now, when you're ready, come up to the house and I'll show you what's what with the chickens.' He banged the door with his hand and then he turned around, pointed his stick and nose toward the house and headed off that way alone. We waited and watched for him to get far enough away so that he couldn't hear us.

'I'm not stepping foot in there!' Walker said.

'We have no choice,' I said, putting my head around the door. The oven looked broken and the place was filthy. The seating area was stained and frayed and the smell was hard to stomach. I pulled my head back and breathed in fresh air. 'Who's going in first?'

'I'll go,' Johnny J said, and he took a deep breath and stepped up into the caravan. Charlie quickly followed. He opened the door to one of the tiny bedrooms – it had a double bed with a dirty duvet and no pillows. He opened the second room to reveal two single bunk beds; one had a blanket, the other didn't. He walked over to the sofa area and lifted off the seat and there was a pull-out bed, but it looked broken.

'This is going to be uncomfortable,' he said.

When we finally all squeezed inside, we stood back to back and side to side like sardines in a tin.

'Will we check out the chickens?' I said. They all agreed. Everyone was itching to get out of the caravan.

The house was cold and dark even though it was a hot day. The old man was sitting by his fire. He heard us approach.

'Ready?'

'Yeah,' I said.

'Good boys,' he said. He didn't mention Charlie. He got up slowly and groaned as he moved, then he rubbed his knees with his long bony fingers. I stayed in the background so he wouldn't grab on to me. He grabbed on to Sumo instead. 'Well, you're a big fella, aren't you? Which one are you?'

I mouthed the word 'Theo'.

'Isn't Theo the small one?' Sumo mumbled.

'What's that?'

'Theo,' Sumo said.

'Good man, Theo,' Jimbo said. 'What age are ya?' he asked.

Sumo looked to me for the answer.

'He's sixteen,' I lied.

'Is that you, Dave?'

'Yeah,' I said.

'Is Theo dumb?' Jimbo said.

'No.'

'Why are you speaking for him?'

'Sorry,' I mumbled.

'Are you blind?' Sumo said.

'Yes,' Jimbo said.

'Cool,' Sumo said, and Jimbo laughed. He told us to pick up some clean bed linen from his hot press and then he pointed his stick in the direction of the chickens and we were off.

36

The Animals

Jimbo headed straight toward the smell. We followed in a line behind him.

When the noise of chicken squawking was really loud and the chickens had us surrounded, he raised his arms in the air.

'Girls, meet the boys,' he said. He was still ignoring Charlie. Nobody said anything. Maybe he'd forgotten she was there and it would be rude to mention it. 'Say hello, boys.'

'Hello,' we said.*

He showed us their feed and how to clean out

---

* 1. Chickens peck, and pecking is the same as biting, except it hurts more.

2. Some chickens run sideways, which is very freaky.

3. A lot of them like to spread their wings and jump/fly into kids' faces.

their henhouse. He also showed us how to collect the eggs. Feeding was fine, cleaning was disgusting, but collecting the eggs was cool. Next he brought us to the cowshed. I'd never seen a real cow before. They were massive and loud and breathed really heavily, and if I hadn't been so mesmerised by their massive eyes and huge wet noses, I would have run for my life.

'Cows meet boys. Boys meet cows,' he said.

Charlie was standing right beside him! She said nothing, so neither did I.

'Ever milked a cow before?'

'Ah we're from Dublin,' Walker said sarcastically.

'Yeah, well, so is Premier Dairies. There are cows in Dublin, believe it or not, Smarty-pants.' Jimbo couldn't see but he was sharp as a tack. Walker *was* a smarty-pants. 'Which one are you?'

'I'm Simon,' Walker said.

'Well, from now on you're Smarty-pants.'

We all laughed. That name suited him better than Simon.

'Who else have I?' Jimbo said.

'Eh, Alvin and Brittany.'

'Oh yes. You ever milked a cow, Alvin?'

'No, sir,' Johnny J said.

251

'No, Jimbo,' Jimbo said.

'No, Jimbo.'

'Right, let me show you how.'

Jimbo felt around for the stool. Charlie moved it closer to him with her foot. He found it and sat. He dropped his stick and grabbed on to the cow's pink soft bits and I felt sick.

'Good morning, Gloria,' he said to the cow.

She mooed a bit, but I think that's because he was kneading her pink bits like my mam kneaded dough.

'I'm giving a little nudge, a push, a prod, just to relax the muscles here, boys. Old Gloria needs to relax and leave the milk down.'

The others moved forward, fascinated. I hung back, disgusted. Charlie looked around.

'There's room here,' she said, and she pulled me closer. *Thanks a lot, Charlie.*

'You ever seen a cow being milked on TV?' Jimbo asked.

Sumo put up his arm. I nudged him. 'What?' Sumo said.

'He can't see, remember?' Walker said.

'Oh yeah, sorry. I did, Mr . . . Jimbo.'

Jimbo started making a pulling motion. 'And they did this? Right?'

'Right,' Sumo said.

'Wrong,' he said. 'To milk a cow you take your thumb and forefinger, you clip them around the top of the udder, then with the other hand you squeeze the milk out. It starts slow but speeds up as old Gloria here relaxes.'

He was doing it with his gnarly alien fingers. By now I felt faint. I didn't say anything. Nobody else seemed bothered by the fact that we were in a barn with a weird old man, a large cow and milk being squeezed into a bucket.

When he finished his demonstration, he asked us, 'Who wants to try?' They all did.

I just hung back.

Johnny J looked back at me. 'You're after me? Yeah?'

'Jeremy, I'll do the cow for you if you do the chickens for me,' Walker said.

I nodded enthusiastically.

'But the cow is way cooler,' Sumo said to me.

'Yeah, but the chickens will set off my allergies and I'll die,' Walker said.

He was right. We were on a farm surrounded by straw, grass and all the other things that set Walker off. He was already looking a little puffy around the eyes.

'Do you have your medicine?' I asked.

'A box of tabs and one inhaler,' he said.

'Is that enough?'

'Hope so,' he said.

After the chickens were fed and the cows were milked, Jimbo showed us the fence with the hole in it.

'Ever fixed a fence?'

You would think by now he'd know the answer. *Of course not!*

'No, Jimbo,' Sumo, Charlie and Johnny J said. Walker and I stayed quiet.

Jimbo got out a hammer and nails and chicken wire, and when he put the first nail in the wood and hammered, it was like watching a daredevil do a trick. I was sure he was going to hammer his long bony alien finger into the wood, but he didn't, and when he was done, he turned to us.*

'Demonstration over. Any questions?'

Nobody spoke.

'Right then, that's for tomorrow. Now, which one of you can make an omelette?'

---

* 1. Back then, adults gave kids hammers and nails to fix fences without a second thought.

2. Kids left the house in the morning and only came back for dinner.

3. It was a very different time.

'Me,' Charlie said.

'Others, collect the eggs. You –' he pointed in Charlie's direction – 'come with me.'

We collected the eggs. There were a lot of eggs, but the hens were moodier second time around; a couple didn't like us picking up their eggs. One snapped at me and another flew into Johnny J's face! It wasn't as cool as I'd first thought, but it was still better than milking a cow.

Earlier that day we were eating ice cream and now we were farm slaves in a place that smelled of every bad thing all at once. Walker sat on the fence, inhaling his inhaler, leaving Johnny J, Sumo and me to do all the hard work. Sumo was happy though – when he took over the egg hunting, he talked to the chickens as he took the eggs from beneath them.

'Hello, lady, what have we here?' Once he'd retrieved the egg or eggs he'd thank the chicken. 'Thanks, lady.'

As we walked back to the caravan, Johnny J spun around, scanning the trees, the green fields, the animals sauntering around, the space and the pink sky. 'It smells bad, but this is amazing,' he said.

'Yeah,' I said, because it was.

Walker just sniffed and wiped his weeping eyes. 'It's all right,' he said. 'Dublin's better though.'

Charlie loved the place too. She didn't have to say it. There were enough trees to keep her climbing for years. In the short time we'd been there she'd already scaled two and was eyeing up a third.

'You know what?' Johnny J said as we walked back to the farmhouse. 'We always talk about adventure. This is adventure.'

I was hoping for spaceships and superheroes, not a day on the farm! But I had to agree it was an adventure. I was just really scared about how the adventure would end.

37

The Meal

That evening, when all the chores were done, Charlie helped Jimbo cook eggs, I cut the brown bread, Johnny J set the table, Sumo made the largest pot of tea I'd ever seen in my life and Walker sat by the turf fire sneezing and holding on to his inhaler.

'You all right, Simon?' I said.

Walker had forgotten his new name was Simon. So had everyone else.

'Hey, Smarty-pants.' I walked over and put my hand on his shoulder.

'What? Oh yeah. What?'

'Are you all right?'

He settled back in the big old armchair, resting

his feet on a large wolfhound that moved so little that if he hadn't farted every five minutes I'd have thought he was dead. Walker nodded. 'Having the time of my life, Dave.' I was worried about his allergies and so was he, but he was pretending everything was fine. I suppose we all were.

The omelette was brilliant. My mam doesn't like eggs, so we never ate them. Charlie and Jimbo put mushrooms and spinach and ham and cheese in there and every bite melted in my mouth. Charlie was a brilliant cook. I did not see that coming. The brown bread came lashed in fresh butter. The tea was way too strong, but with enough sugar it tasted really good. We all sat around the big old wooden table on long benches and savaged the food in front of us.

The radio was on, and when Jimbo wasn't shouting at the men talking politics, he was telling us stories about the way things used to be. His stories weren't boring at all. He was funny, and when he talked about his dead wife, Denise, he'd chuckle to himself.* He'd laugh at

---

* 1. She used to fall asleep in that chair and belch like a champion.
  2. Her farts were so loud she'd wake the dog.
  3. The dog would jump up and run into the wall.

his own stories. We all laughed too. Jimbo's hands and aged appearance didn't freak me out as much in the dim light. By the end of the meal I realised that Jimbo wasn't mean or angry – he was kind and funny and I really liked him. He didn't ask us questions. He said that if we wanted to call our parents, the phone was in the hall. He warned us not to stay on it long though because phone calls to Dublin cost a lot. We said we didn't need to call anyone. He didn't push it. He did wonder how long we were planning on staying in Wexford.

'Two weeks,' I said.

'Two weeks here with me?' he said.

'If that's all right, Jimbo,' Johnny J said.

He nodded to himself. 'Well, that's just fine.'

It had been a long day and we were a million miles from home, but we were warm, and fed, and we had jobs and a place to stay, even if it did smell of petrol, burnt toast, a little bit of poo, a lot of wee and lavender.

We ran across the field to our new home, and although it was dark it was still warm out, so we grabbed the fresh linen and we all lay on the grass looking up at the stars.

'What do you think is happening at home?' Sumo said.

'My mam and dad will be doing the war dance,' I said.

Sumo was deeply sad. 'My mam will be crying.'

Walker was seriously anxious. 'Well, I'm a dead man. My mam will have called my three sisters home, and you know what they're like.'

He was right. His life wouldn't be worth living.

'What about you, Charlie?' Johnny J asked. 'What do you think is going on?'

'My brother Louis went missing for a whole day once. My mam, Ben and Sean looked everywhere for him. Mam was terrified, but she kept saying everything would be fine; she knew it would all work out. I'd like to think she knows everything will be all right.'

'Where did your brother go?' I asked.

'A concert in Slane Castle,' she said.

'What we did is way worse,' I said.

'Oh yeah,' she said. 'I'm a dead girl walking.'

We all laughed. Charlie could be really funny. I wondered why I hadn't noticed that before.

'What about you, Johnny J?' Charlie asked.

'I'm just worried, but I'm always just worried,'

he said, and I knew what he meant. His eyes glistened under the moonlight. *Is he going to cry? Nah, Johnny J doesn't cry. It's just the light.*

'Goodnight, Dave,' Johnny J said.

I laughed. 'Goodnight, Alvin.'

'Goodnight, chipmunks,' he said to Sumo, Walker and Charlie.

'Goodnight, Alvin,' they said, and giggled.

And that's where we fell asleep, right there under a million stars.

38

The Work

We woke the next morning to a new day of sun and hard work, and hard work can take your mind off anything – well, pretty much anything. I still thought about prison and my mam's disappointment all the time, but my stomach felt better and the fresh air helped me cope, and seeing as there was an old rubber tyre shoved into the caravan loo, doing my business outside encouraged me to be quick and efficient. There was no time to sit on a toilet and feel sorry for myself.

Charlie and Walker nominated themselves to clean out the caravan. Betty Bloomers came up the road in a truck with some cleaning products and a bundle of clean sheets and blankets. Johnny J and I spent the morning fixing the fence and Sumo took on all the chicken and cow duties. Jimbo was never far away. The fridge was stacked with lemonade, milk and cheese, and the larder was jam-packed full of brown bread and scones. We could snack when we wanted, which meant that Sumo spent a lot of time in the kitchen.

'I think these scones are even better than Spam sandwiches,' he said.

'Dirt on the ground is better than Spam sandwiches,' I said.

It was Saturday 23 June 1990, and it was glorious. Normally on a Saturday I'd spend my morning helping my mam with the shopping or reading a book in bed or cycling around the place looking to see if the lads were up and around. Some Saturdays I spent alone in Sumo's den, playing on the computer or reading his stacks of comics, but on this Saturday I was on a farm in Wexford, fixing a fence with my very best friend in the world. Aside from being wanted criminals, it felt good.

'Who's cooler – Indiana Jones or James Bond?'*

---

* 1. James Bond is a spy with a licence to kill.
  2. Indiana Jones is a professor with a bullwhip.
  3. We were nerds when it came to spy and adventure movies.

'Indiana,' Johnny J said.

'Are you sure? Bond's pretty cool.'

'Yeah, but he has to wear suits. Indy wears what he likes,' he said.

It was a very good point. Technically, suits were not cool, even on James Bond. 'Yeah, I think you're right, although Indy is a teacher and Bond is a spy so . . .'

'Yeah, but Indy finds treasure and Bond just kills people.'

Excellent point. 'OK, Indy it is then. How about who would win in a fight?'

'Bond,' he said.

'Yeah, definitely Bond – he's vicious,' I said. 'Although Indy is brilliant at distraction and escape techniques.'

'True, but no one escapes Bond.'

'Yeah, but if Indy escapes and stays alive, I think in those circumstances it's a kind of win.'

He thought about that. 'Yeah you're right. They're even.'

We talked a lot about stuff like that and zombies. 'Who in our group would be the first to be eaten by zombies?' I asked.

'Sumo,' he said without even thinking. He

hammered a nail into wood as he spoke. 'He's slow and there's a lot of eating on him. Also he'd probably refuse to fight back. He'd probably worry that the brain-eating zombies might have feelings.'

I laughed. 'Yeah.'

'What about Charlie?' I asked, and he stopped hammering.

'I think she'd do fine. She'd probably live in the trees, and she's fast. And I think if she had to, she'd kill as many as she could.'

'You like her,' I said.

'I don't know. She's different. I just like hanging out with her. You know.'

A week earlier I wouldn't have known, but having spent time with her, I was starting to understand.

'But do you *like* her?' I said, and he just gave me a look.

'Why?'

'No reason, just asking,' I said.

'Well, don't.'

'So you do.'

'Shut up and hammer,' he said.

We both shut up for a while, and I was steaming because I knew deep down he liked her and she definitely liked him and I wondered why it bothered me so much. *Who cares?* I thought to myself. *Who really cares?*

I did.

After a while he asked who would win in a fight between a vampire and the Terminator. Now that was a really good question. A vampire against a machine! We talked about that for a really long time and didn't come up with a definitive answer.

By lunchtime the fence was fixed. When we got back to the caravan, the smell of petrol, burnt toast, a little bit of poo, a lot of wee and lavender had been replaced by a mix of bleach and lemon. In the sheds and fields, the cows were milked, the chickens cleaned out and fed and the eggs collected. Jimbo was so happy he treated us to a large lunch of cold meats, brown bread and chips that he fried in a pan with oil on his huge stove. I thought blind men shouldn't mess with fire, but he told me he was only ninety per cent blind, and anyway he'd been making chips that way since he was a boy. The radio was on and the commentators were talking about the Cameroon v Colombia and Czechoslovakia v Costa Rica matches later that evening.

266

'I played football myself back in the day, boys,' Jimbo said.

'No way, Jimbo! Were you deadly at it?' Sumo said. I'd gotten used to seeing him wear the Wookie mask and it didn't even seem to bother him in the sun.

'God, no, I was terrible. My Denise was a better player than I was.'

'Oh. Sorry to hear that, Jimbo,' Sumo said.

'Don't be sorry – I was brilliant at everything else,' he said, and he laughed to himself and we all laughed because his laugh was very funny to listen to. Charlie described it as a mix between a sneeze and a dirty chuckle.

When we were all stuffed, Jimbo went to the loo. 'Excuse me, boys,' he said. 'The throne awaits.'

'The throne,' I said.

'Yeah, he means the loo. That's what my dad calls it too,' Walker said. 'My mam always calls him a thick when he says it.'

We were finishing cleaning the dishes when the news came on. We weren't listening, not really. I was busy washing, Johnny J was drying, Charlie was cleaning the floor, Sumo was wiping down the table, Walker was pretending his allergies were at him and sitting by the fire. We were all making lots of noise, but in the background I heard them mention a manhunt for the 'Fearless Five', but as soon as it was mentioned, Jimbo came in and turned off the radio.

'Now, boys, you've done a fine morning's work, so follow me.'

We followed him outside, and he pointed his stick due south.

'The beach is that way, boys,' he said. 'Follow the smell of the sea and enjoy yourselves. Be back at five for the cows and chickens and don't drown.' We were so excited at the prospect of swimming at the beach that it never occurred to me that Johnny J, Sumo, Walker, Charlie and I were the Fearless Five!

39

The Beach

We ran toward the sea and didn't stop until we got there.

We didn't have swimming togs. All we had was the clothes on our backs and our coats. It had been so nice sleeping outside and the coats made for good pillows. We had nothing to wash ourselves with either, and because it was so hot we were a little bit smelly. Now, if Charlie hadn't been there we would have taken off our jeans and T-shirts and run straight into the water in our pants, but because she was there we stopped at the glistening water's edge and we all looked at one another. *What to do? What to do?*

'Let's just go for it,' Johnny J said.

'Fully clothed?' I said.

'At least it might clean our clothes,' Walker said.

Sumo smelled himself. 'Yeah, I could do with that, lads – not going to lie to you.'

'I'm in,' Charlie said, and before she'd uttered the word 'in', she was already waist-deep in the glistening water and then she disappeared under it head first and I held my breath until she burst back out with her arms spread wide.

'What are you waiting for, boys?' she said, and that was it. I was in. I ran until it was deep enough to dive, and suddenly I was under the cold water, my body tingling from head to toe. I could hear and feel the thunder of the sea and it was exhilarating. When I opened my eyes, I was facing Johnny J. He gave me the thumbs up and for one second the world seemed to stand completely still. Walker hid his spectacles behind a rock and he inched in slowly, holding on to himself, shivering and talking about how cold it was.

'Oh, it's seriously cold . . . Oh, oh, oh, oh, oh, oh no. Oh no . . .'

Sumo walked straight in and up to his chest. Then he just stood there, in his Wookie mask, rubbing at his clothes, turning around every now

270

and then and jumping to avoid waves. He also counselled Walker from his standing position.

'Doing great, Walker. Keep coming, keep coming, keep coming.'

'Oh, shut up, Sumo,' Walker would say every few minutes.

'Any minute now you'll be up to your knees.'

I loved swimming in the canal in Dublin, but the sea was just bliss. Johnny J, Charlie and I splashed around for a bit, until Walker had finally made it to his waist, but by then our clothes were really heavy.

'I'm getting rid of my clothes,' Johnny J said.

'Me too,' Charlie said.

I didn't know what to think. I definitely wasn't going nude. Charlie was there! Not to mention the beach was packed with people of all ages.

They both ran out of the water, past Sumo and Walker, and they stripped off on the beach. Johnny J stripped off to his boxer shorts and she stripped down too. She was wearing A BRA! They ran back into the water, past Walker and Sumo again, who didn't seem to notice she was wearing a bra. They were too busy talking about the problem of Sumo's purple face.

271

'Maybe if I wash it in the salt water.'

'Won't work,' Walker said.

'Why not.'

'The whole point is you can't wash it off.'

'So I'm stuck wearing a Wookie mask for the rest of my life?' Sumo didn't even sound that upset.*

'Nah, your skin will regenerate in twenty-seven days.'

'How do you know?'

'I'm a genius.'

'If you were a genius, you would have known about the dye pack and I wouldn't be standing here wearing a Wookie mask,' Sumo said, and Walker laughed.

'I suppose that is a fact,' he said.

Johnny J and Charlie both dived and started swimming for the horizon. It looked really fun and my clothes were weighing me down, so after I'd really thought about it I waded past the two boys.

'All right, Dave,' Sumo said as I passed him.

'You can call me Jeremy when Jimbo's not around.'

_____

* 1. Sumo wore a Superman cape for an entire summer when he was eight.

2. He dressed as Batman every year on his birthday.

3. In the winter when it was really cold he wore a fur hat with pom-poms that his mother made in her home-economics class in the 1970s.

272

'Nah, it's too confusing,' he said.

'You stripping as well?' Walker said, and there was a hint of alarm in his voice.

'It's the only way,' I said.

Back on the beach I stripped off, but it was only when my trousers were around my ankles that I remembered I was wearing Papa Smurf jocks. *Oh no.*

Walker noticed them straight away, pointed and laughed. 'Hey, Sumo, would you look at Smurfette over there.' Sumo laughed. It was too late to try to peel on my soaking jeans, so I put my T-shirt back on because it was just about long enough to cover Papa Smurf. Then I just ignored the lads and returned to the sea as quickly as my skinny white freckled legs would take me.

Walker was finally up to his chest and washing himself and his clothes, much like Sumo. As I ran past them, Walker started to sing the Smurf song and Sumo joined in. Walker took off Papa Smurf's voice and he kept repeating the phrase 'Smurf along with me'. It was really annoying.

In my head I angrily told my mam what I thought about all of this. *I'm not six years old, Mam. Why do you insist on buying me jocks with Smurfs on*

them? Yes, I liked them for a really long time, but I'm
thirteen years old! I need jocks like Johnny J's – just
black or white or even blue. Another thing, Mam,
where do you even get jocks for thirteen-years-olds
with Smurfs on them?

I swam out to Johnny J and Charlie; they were just treading water together in what felt like the middle of the ocean. They were too far out to sea to notice that I had Papa Smurf's face on my jocks. I made a mental note to stay in the water until they had dressed and gone. I wasn't going to let Johnny J or Charlie see that.

They were laughing at something when I swam up to them. 'What's so funny?'

'Ah nothing,' Charlie said, and she laughed again and then Johnny J laughed.

'Nothing is never funny,' I said.

'You had to be here,' Charlie said.

'I am here.'

'A few minutes ago,' Johnny J said, so I let it go.

'Right,' I said, and I was hurt. Less than a few weeks ago it would have been Johnny J and me in a little huddle together enjoying a private joke, and now Charlie was in and I was out. I swam on.

Neither of them tried to call me back. They just stayed treading water and whispering into one another's ears. It was easy to see that I wasn't wanted, so I just swam away from them and talked to myself in my head. *So that's the way you want it. Fine. We can all be like that. I can go off with* . . . But that was the thing. I couldn't go off with anyone. I could see Walker on Sumo's shoulders in the near distance. They weren't missing me either; they had their own thing going. Johnny J and Charlie definitely weren't missing me. I was alone. Worse than that, I was a lone fugitive. I wanted to cry but I didn't. Instead I just treaded water and repeated the words *Don't do it. Do not cry* in my head. Then I thought about things and it made me mad. *After all I've done for him! This is the thanks I get. Ah, ah, ah, I can feel a tear. Stop! Stop it! Too late.* Tears raced down my wet face, so I splashed myself and dunked my head underwater and stayed there stewing for as long as my lungs would allow.

When I finally surfaced it was in time to see Johnny J walk onto the beach. Charlie was still treading water where I'd left them. Johnny J foraged in a bag and took out some cans and munched into a bar of chocolate. Sumo and Walker soon joined him. Charlie lay on her back and floated silently.

I thought about joining the lads, but I was still too angry with Johnny J to share a bar of chocolate with him or drink from the same can. Instead I just bobbed up and down, my eyes darting from the boys eating to Charlie floating. They all seemed so happy. I wanted to scream, *It's just not fair.*

I don't know for how long I was looking away, maybe it was thirty seconds, maybe it was a whole minute, but when I looked back in Charlie's direction, she was gone.

40

The Hero

I started to swim toward where Charlie had last been floating, and then I saw her. She was barely visible and thrashing. I called out to her but she didn't respond. She was in trouble. She disappeared under again. My heart twisted in my chest.

'It's OK, Charlie,' I shouted, 'I'm coming. Don't panic, OK?' I moved as quickly as I could. She was wild in the water. I inched closer and I remembered my water-safety trainer's advice. 'Don't climb on me. OK?'*

---

* 1. A drowning victim's first reaction will be to climb on top of you.
  2. Use a buoy, or if you don't have one use a T-shirt or a towel.
  3. Only get close enough to throw it and tell the drowning person to grab on.

I wasn't sure that she could hear me, she was really struggling. I was nearly beside her now. I didn't have a buoy, but I was still wearing my T-shirt. I ripped it off and twisted it into a sort of rope. She was struggling, gurgling and slipping under. I threw it to her.

'Charlie, grab on.' She flailed around and I moved closer and she grabbed it. I pulled her toward me. 'I've got you,' I said. 'Just hold on.'

I moved in a straight line back to shore, just like my trainer had taught me. I looked back every few strokes to make sure she was still holding on but always keeping a safe distance. We were nearly back to shore before the boys realised that something was wrong.

Johnny J was the first to reach us. He helped me carry Charlie onto the sand. She dropped to the ground. Her lips were a mix of purple and blue. I thought robbing was terrifying, but that was the most scared I'd ever been. My heart raced in my chest and my hands shook.

'Call an ambulance,' I said, and I rolled her onto her side. Johnny J's mam had forced him to do the same course as me, so he was busy checking her airway, breathing and circulation.

She coughed and spluttered and raised her hands.

'Don't call an ambulance,' she said, but it was in a hoarse whisper that worried me.

'I think we should,' I said.

Johnny J looked worried too, but then she sat up and breathed in and out slowly and steadily.

'If I go to hospital, we're done for,' she said. 'I'm fine, really I am.' Then she looked at me and she smiled with her purple-blue lips. 'Thanks, Jeremy, you're my hero,' she said, and even though I was wearing Papa Smurf shorts on a crowded beach in front of everyone, it felt really good to be called a hero.

'You're welcome,' I said, and we just looked at one another for a few seconds. I blushed and I looked away first, but it felt nice. Then she started crying, I mean really crying. I didn't even know Charlie was capable of that kind of loud, snotty, full-on ugly-face crying.

Johnny J hugged her and told her everything would be fine, and when she got up to walk back to the caravan, she walked away with him. I'd saved her but she left with him. As I watched them go, my chest tightened a little. Walker couldn't believe what had just happened.

'This is all mad,' he said, 'totally mad.' He boxed Sumo on the arm. 'Chips?' Walker said.

'Oh yeah,' Sumo said.

They didn't ask me; I don't know if they just expected me to go with them or if they even noticed I was there. They just walked off and I was left alone on the beach in my Papa Smurf jocks. It was depressing.

I didn't feel like going back to the caravan. I lay on the beach and let my T-shirt and jocks dry. Even though it was hot it took a long time and my T-shirt was stuck together with sand. I brushed it down, and when I finally got my wet jeans on, I walked up and down the beach for a long time, watching people come and go, scratching and shaking sand from my back, front, sides and armpits and thinking about my family at home in Dublin. My mam was probably going insane. I missed her. I missed her cooking and I missed her washing my clothes. *How am I supposed to get sand out of my T-shirt?*

I missed her smile and laugh and even the way she shouted. I missed my dad too. He'd be upset because my mam was upset. He couldn't bear to see her sad. In my head I could see him pacing up and down the hall corridor the way he always did when he was worried, sad, frustrated or scared.

I wondered what Rich was thinking. I thought about how I'd feel if Rich robbed garages. I'd be worried. Maybe he was worried too. It was a pity Johnny J would probably be incarcerated somewhere. That would mess up the band. I missed Rich. *Weird*. I hoped Rachel wouldn't stay home with the family to mind my parents, because she needed to go back to nursing school. It was important to her.

I thought about my friends and the trouble we were in. Charlie could have died. If she had, it would have been my fault because she wouldn't have been in that water if she hadn't robbed a garage and a security van and run away with us. I was supposed to be going into secondary school in September, but now my friends and I would be heading into some kids' detention centre. I was angry at the world and God and myself, Auntie Alison and Johnny J and even poor Mrs Tulsi. I thought about running away for good, from everything and everyone – my friends, family, jail, life. But I couldn't. There was nowhere to go and nothing to do but wait. So I walked back to the caravan with a head full of sand and a heavy heart.

41

The Fight

It was nearly dark when I made it back to the
caravan. The boys were sitting around the table
playing a game of snap. Charlie was wrapped up
in some of Betty Bloomers' blankets on the bed,
with the door open so that she could see the boys
and they could see her. She was still pretty shaken
up after nearly drowning. I walked up to the door
of her little bleach-and-lemon-smelling room.

'You OK?' I asked.

'I'm fine,' she said. 'Thanks.' She sniffed. Her
eyes were raw. It looked like she was still on the
verge of tears. It made me sad as well as angry. It
wasn't a good mix of emotions.

'Where were you?' Johnny J asked.

'Like you'd care,' I said.

'What?' he said, and he laughed. That really hurt. 'What's wrong with you?' he asked.

What's wrong with me? Oh, I don't know. Maybe I'm frightened and lonely and upset and sick and lost and tired and . . . I couldn't think of anything else.

'What's wrong with *you*?' I shouted.

Walker shoved his glasses to the bridge of his swollen nose and sat up straight. Sumo stared at me blankly through his Wookie mask. They weren't that sure what was happening. I wasn't sure myself. I just felt all this rage deep down in the pit of my sick stomach.

Johnny J stood up from the table to face me. 'Nothing, I'm fine,' he said.

'Yeah, well, good, because you're the only one,' I said.

Sumo raised his purple hand in the air. 'I'm fine too,' he said.

'No, you're not, Sumo. You, me, Walker and Charlie are in big trouble. We've done a terrible thing.' It was the first time I'd said it out loud. It was the first time I'd admitted it to myself. WE'D DONE A TERRIBLE THING.

Walker and Sumo dropped their heads. Charlie said nothing. I had my back to her so I couldn't see her reaction.

'I did what you did,' Johnny J said, and he wasn't so cocky-sounding any more.

'Your mam is sick, so everyone will feel sorry for you. It's the rest of us that have really taken a chance here.'

Walker squeezed his head between his hands. 'Why didn't I think of that? He's right, you know,' he said to Sumo. 'We're dead. I'll never be a Young Scientist in my own right. Thanks a lot, Johnny J.' He lay his head on the table and banged it gently against it three times for dramatic effect. 'My life is over.' He was careful not to inflict further damage to his nose.

'It's your fault too, Walker! If you hadn't insisted on robbing the security van! WHAT WERE YOU THINKING?' I screamed.

'YOU STARTED THIS!' He was shouting now too. It was a good point.

'Jeremy, why are you saying all this?' Charlie said, and I turned to face her.

Charlie sat up in the bed, but she kept the blankets wrapped around her, hugging them close. Her wild red hair was a mess, but at least her lips weren't purple and blue, even though they weren't a normal colour either.

'YOU COULD HAVE DIED TODAY,' I shouted 'YOU NEARLY DROWNED, AND YOUR MAM, DAD AND BROTHERS DON'T EVEN KNOW WHERE YOU ARE.'

She recoiled in the bed and started crying again.

If they wanted to, Charlie's brothers could kick the colours of the rainbow out of any of us, even Sumo, and if she had died they would be right to. I wouldn't blame them.

Charlie was lucky to be alive. I was lucky not to have drowned myself. I wasn't a hero or even a gung-ho gangster. I was just a stupid kid, a really very stupid kid. We all were! And I felt sick that it was my fault. I was angry at them for listening to me and at the world for making Mrs Tulsi sick and at Auntie Alison for threatening to take away my best friend.

Johnny J's face had changed colour from his usual cool caramel colour to a beetroot red. Walker stopped banging his head against the table and he was just still, eyes wide and like a dead fish. I couldn't tell what Sumo was thinking under the Wookie mask.

'He's right, we're all stupid,' Walker said.

Sumo had his hand on Walker's back and every now and then he'd pat it.

'We shouldn't have done any of this,' Johnny J shouted.

'No, we shouldn't,' I shouted back.

Johnny J stormed out of the caravan. Charlie scrambled to disentangle herself from the blankets. I was just standing there in the middle of the tiny caravan in shock. It was the first fight Johnny J and I had ever had and it was horrible.

'He's your best friend,' Charlie said to me as she squeezed past me. Then she ran out the door to find Johnny J. I turned to face the two boys.

'Sorry,' I said.

'We're dead,' Walker mumbled.

'It's still worth it if we save Johnny J's mam, right?' Sumo said.

'What if we don't, Sumo?' I said. She was so sick and I wondered what if it was too late? I worried it would be for nothing.

'Ah no, she'll be grand,' Sumo said. 'Everything will be grand.'

Walker started banging his head gently on the table again. When I knew the coast was clear and

286

Johnny J and Charlie were nowhere to be seen, I left the caravan. I walked toward the village. It was dark by the time I reached it. I'd missed dinner back at the farmhouse; I was starving. I walked into the chipper.

'I'll have a burger and chips, please,' I said, and I handed him all the money I had in my pocket. He handed me a pound back. I made a mental note of how much the burger and chips cost so Walker could note it in his notebook. We needed to keep an eye on money if it was going to last the full two weeks.

The chipper had big orange plastic seats and white plastic tables lining one wall. Over the seating area was a clock. It read 10.30 p.m. I sat below the clock waiting for my food. I noticed a newspaper on the seat opposite. It was crumpled and slightly torn, but I grabbed it because the spotty teenager behind the counter wasn't talkative and I was bored listening to my own angry thoughts. One minute I was still shouting at Johnny J in my head and the next I was begging him to forgive me. It was exhausting. The front page was all about the Irish team and the big game against Romania they had in front of them.

It was the match that would determine whether or not they'd get into the World Cup quarter-finals and it was a huge deal. Not to me though. I had much bigger things to worry about, like losing my best friend and destroying my entire future. There was something about the brilliant weather on page 2 and then boring politics stuff on pages 3 and 4. Something terrible had happened in a country I'd never even heard of on page 5, and then I turned to page 6 and my heart skipped a beat. I was looking at the photo that Sumo's mam took of us standing in Sumo's garden wearing our football-supporter disguises, and the headline above it read 'Have you seen the Fearless Five?' *Oh, it's us!*

With trembling heart, hands, feet, legs, body and mind I read on. It mentioned our names, ages, where we lived, our parents, our school, everything about us!* And then it told the world, or at least the whole of Ireland, what we'd done in a lot of detail. The article asked people to keep an eye out

---

* 1. They spelled my name Jermy. Rich thought that was hilarious and tried to get the nickname Germy Jeremy going. It went nowhere.

  2. Charlie was referred to as 'him' halfway through the article. She didn't seem to mind.

  3. Walker was described as a little sickly fella and he went nuts.

for us and then it gave the number of a police station to contact.

The spotty teen handed me my burger. I hid my face.

'Thanks,' I mumbled.

'Whatever,' he said.

The article ended with a plea from our parents for all of us to come home. My guts twisted. I had a lot to think about. Our faces were in the paper! We had an outlaw name! *The Fearless Five*. The whole country was looking for us. It wouldn't be long before they found us. Jimbo being blind was in our favour. At least he couldn't identify us. Betty Bloomers could see though. Maybe she didn't read the newspaper. I hoped not. My mam didn't. She said all news was bad news so she only did crosswords. I didn't know what to do. If I told the others it would probably only make things worse. I decided to sleep on it.

I tore the article out of the paper, folded it and put it in the back pocket of my jeans. I pushed my burger and chips away. I stood up, brushed myself down and walked toward the door.

The spotty teen shouted at me, 'Hey, you didn't even touch that food!'

'Whatever,' I said, pushing the swinging door open and swaggering down the road. I was one of the Fearless Five!

When I reached the caravan it was quiet. Everyone was sleeping. I just grabbed one of Betty Bloomers' blankets and went outside. I liked sleeping under the stars, even though it was a little cold. I hugged the blankets close and counted as many stars as I could. After a lot of counting I realised that for the first time since I'd started this whole thing I wasn't afraid. I wasn't scared at all. I know it sounds crazy, but seeing our photo in the paper was a relief. It reminded me that all the madness would soon be over. Whatever was going to happen would happen and there was nothing I could do about it. My mam used to sing me a song when I was a kid. It was called 'Que Sera Sera'. It was supposed to be French or Italian or Spanish, although Dad said it wasn't any of those languages (he'd got the answer wrong in a pub quiz), but anyway the song said 'What will be will be'. That's what I went to sleep singing in my head. *What will be will be.*

42

The Secret

I woke up outside to the sounds of birds squawking. I wasn't sure if they were happy, sad, friendly or fighting, but it hurt my ears.

'They're loud, aren't they?' Charlie said, and suddenly she was looming over me and it gave me a start. It was still really early. Yellow sun burst from what appeared to be a silver crack between the blue sky and the white clouds.

I jumped up into a sitting position, fixed my messy hair into a tight ponytail and popped the pen and pencil that lay on the ground back into it, then I wiped sleep from my eyes and sniffed to clear my stuffy head. She sat down beside me and crossed her legs the way my mam did when she was doing her yoga poses.

'It beautiful here, isn't it?' she said, looking at the sky.

'Yeah,' I said.

'Are you OK?' she said.

I hunched. 'I'm grand,' I said.

'You're not acting like you're grand.'

'It doesn't matter anyway,' I said. 'We'll be going home soon.'

'What do you mean?'

I pulled the piece of newspaper from my back pocket and handed it to her. 'We're done for,' I said.

She looked at it and her eyes widened. 'The Fearless Five?!' she gasped, and then she smiled a little. 'That's so cool.'

'I know, but it means they are looking for us outside Dublin,' I said solemnly.

'Wow, we're like real gangsters.'

'I was thinking outlaws.'

'Yeah, outlaws is better.'

'What's going to happen to you when we get caught?' I asked.

'Same thing as you, I suppose.'

'At least if they put us in some boys' detention centre we'll be together.'

'Maybe not. Maybe they'll separate you,' she said.

'I'll probably end up sharing a room with a gurrier called Stab-a-Rasher,' I said.

'I'll probably be better off in a girls' detention centre than at home, cos my brothers will kill me.'

'What about your mam and dad?'

'My brothers are scarier.'

'I heard they were scared of you,' I said.

'Oh, they are,' she said.

'Oh. My sister's scary too,' I said.

'Yeah?' she said.

'Once she banged the door so hard it came off its hinges.'

Charlie smiled. 'Sean kicked a hole through one of ours. My mam dragged him upstairs by his ear.'

'My mam drags Rich down the stairs by the ear all the time,' I said, and we both laughed at the image. Then we became quiet and we both sat staring at the day breaking in front of our eyes.

'We can't give up,' she said after a while.

'It would be better for us if we did,' I said.

'We need to lay low for at least another week,' she said.

'How do we even know that Johnny J's mam is going to use the ticket?'

'We don't, but if we give ourselves up before Mrs Tulsi has a chance to use that ticket, they will take it off her,' Charlie said.

I nodded. She was right.

'We're in big trouble no matter what, so let's not give up on her yet,' Charlie went on.

'OK, I won't. I promise.'

'And, Jeremy, I think you're brilliant,' she said, and I blushed so deeply I thought my head would explode. *Stupid face.*

'I used to think you were mean, but I was wrong about you,' she said.

In that moment I realised I liked Charlie Eastman. *OH NO!*

'I was wrong about you too,' I said, and now I was purple! *Stupid, stupid face.**

'So we'll stick together?' she said.

---

* 1. I'd never liked a girl before.
  2. It made me want to puke and at the same time jump around.
  3. I didn't like it, but at the same time I did.

'Yeah,' I promised. 'We'll stay close to the farm – no more beach trips,' I said, and she smiled and agreed it was best to stay with Jimbo on his farm, surrounded by nothing but fields, fences and animals.

'Besides, I don't feel like drowning again any time soon.'

'You didn't drown,' I said.

'Thanks to you. Anyway, Jimbo has a list of jobs as long as his arm,' she said. She handed me back the newspaper. 'Let's not say it to the others.'

I nodded. Walker would lose it and Johnny J felt bad enough already. I felt terrible about our argument. I kept saying sorry to him in my head. I'd folded the article back up and put it back in my pocket.

'Our secret,' I said, and she nodded. 'Where are you going?' I asked.

'Back to bed,' she said, and waved me goodbye, and she walked into the caravan and quietly closed the door.

43
The Truth

I couldn't go back to sleep, so I got up and shook the last of the sand out of my T-shirt and I walked as far as the farmhouse and I grinned the whole way there.*

Jimbo was up and in his kitchen boiling his kettle. I hadn't eaten the previous night so I was ravenous. I walked in the door and he immediately asked who was there.

'It's me Jer—' *Uh-oh, I'm supposed to be called Dave.* 'Rave. I mean Dave.'

---

* 1. I knew Johnny J'd hate me.
  2. I hoped he'd forgive me, but I guessed he wouldn't.
  3. I'd been scared a lot by then, but that was the most scared I'd ever been.

'Ah, Dave, and where are the other chipmunks?'

'Oh, Dave wasn't a chipmunk,' I said, and then I realised he knew we'd been lying about our names. 'You know the chipmunks?'

'I have grandchildren,' he said.

'Oh.'

'Are you alone?' he asked.

'Everyone else is in bed.'

'Good. Now, I'm going to make tea and you'll put on some bacon and we'll have a little chat about what happens next,' he said.

My heart sank. *He knows.* 'How did you know?'

'My Betty saw you all in the paper last night.'

'We're not real robbers,' I said. 'You needn't be scared.'

He laughed. 'I'm scared of a lot of things, boy, but you and your friends don't make the list.'

The pan was sizzling. 'Go on, drop the bacon in the pan,' he said. 'As soon as it turns pink, flip it. Then when the other side pinks up, turn it again and do that until the fat's nice and charred.'

'What's charred?'

'It's not burnt – that's what charred is.'

'That's helpful.'

'Crispy not snappy,' he said, rubbing his fingers

together. It still didn't make much sense, but I said, 'OK,' anyway.

'And put on some toast while you're at it.'

'But I'm watching the bacon.'

'I can make tea, watch bacon and make toast all at the same time, and I'm a blind old man,' he said.

'How do you watch bacon?' I asked.

'With my fingers,' he said.

'Gross,' I mumbled, and I ran across the kitchen to pop four slices of bread in the biggest toaster I'd ever seen. Then I ran back and sighed with relief – the bacon was fine, still pink.

'Is it charring?' he asked.

'I think so,' I said, turning it with a fork. He lifted the pot of tea and counted seven steps to the table. I could see him counting with his mouth. He set it down. Then he took a deep sniff of the air.

'Nearly there,' he said. He felt one of the cups, and once he knew exactly where it was placed on the table, he poured the tea into it. He somehow filled it just the right amount. Then he did the same to the second.

'Do you like milk?' he said, feeling for the jug of milk on the table.

298

'I can do it,' I said, but he'd poured milk into the two teas before I had time to move. The toast popped up and the bacon seemed ready.

'Let's go,' he said.

I plated up the bacon and the bread. He took a deep sniff of it when I put it on the table.

'Bacon sandwiches have to be my favourite thing in the world,' he said.

We made up our own sandwiches. Jimbo put way too much butter on his, but when he smelled me putting ketchup on mine, he called me a philistine.

'What does that mean?'

'It means there is an art to making a bacon sandwich, and ketchup is not a part of that art.'

'It is in Dublin.'

'Philistines,' he said.

I took a bite out of my sandwich. It tasted so good I wished the moment would last forever. If it did it would mean that Jimbo wouldn't say what I knew he was going to say, but the moment passed. He cleared his throat. *Here it comes* . . .

'What am I going to say?' he said.

'You're going to say that you have to call the guards,' I said, and I made up my mind to escape.

I'd finish the sandwich, then I'd run to the caravan. I'd wake up the others and we'd run away and hide. It would be difficult but we could do it. I knew we could.

'No. I'm not calling the guards.'

'Really?'

'You are.'

'Can't,' I said.

'You're going to get caught, boy.'

'I know.'

'So?'

'We just have to wait another week or so.'

'How's that?'

'Johnny J's mam is really sick.'

'Which one is Johnny J?'

'Alvin,' I said.

'How sick?'

'The chemo isn't working. They say she's dying.'

'Oh,' he said, and suddenly he seemed so sad. 'I'm sorry.'

'It's OK, we're going to save her,' I said.

'By stealing money?'

'We bought her a plane ticket to America. We have to wait until the travel agent posts it to her, and she needs a visa too, but when she gets there,

Walker – that's Simon/Smarty-pants to you – he says they can save her.'

Jimbo put down his sandwich and he sighed deeply.

'So that's what this is all about?'

'Yeah.'

'Oh, Dave.'

'It's Jeremy. My name is Jeremy.'

'Oh, Jeremy, I'm very sorry for your friend's troubles.'

'Thanks, but it's going to be OK if we can just stay here for a while longer.'

'I wish that was true. I wish I could help you save your friend's mother. I wish that she'd jump on a plane to America and they would save her and she'd return good as new, but that's not possible, boy.'

'Why?' I asked, and I felt my eyes start to burn and my chest start to hurt.

'Because if she is as sick as you say, she's going nowhere, and even if she could travel, it's too late.'

'How do you know?'

Then he rubbed what looked like a small tear from his eye. 'The chemo stopped working for my Denise too.'

'I'm sorry.'

'Thank you.'

'But your wife didn't have us. She didn't have America – no offence.'

'None taken, and you're right she didn't have you, but she had me and she had Betty and we would have gone to the moon and back to save her if it could have helped. Do you believe that, Jeremy?'

'I do,' I said. Jimbo was a really nice man. I know he wouldn't lie to me.

'But there is nothing that anyone can do, not here, not in America, once the chemo stops working.'

'You're saying that Johnny J's mam is going to die?' I said, and my eyes were suddenly full, my face hot and my ears sore.

'I am, boy,' he said. 'And I'm very, very sorry for that.'

'Oh,' I said, and then I was crying, and when he put his arms out, I walked straight into them. I didn't even notice his long alien fingers. I just sobbed into his nice clean shirt. When I was cried out, Jimbo explained that it was very important that Johnny J spent no more time away from his mother.

'She needs him with her now,' he said, and it made sense.

'OK.'

'Tell you what – seeing as you missed all the matches, why don't you, me, Betty, the boys, Brittany and my grandkids go to Peter's pub for the match this evening.'

'Brittany's real name is Charlie. And what about the guards?'

'You leave that to me. I'll talk to them and explain things, but we can have one more day together, can't we?' he said.

'That would be brilliant,' I said. Ireland would be playing Romania later that evening, and if we won, Ireland would qualify for the quarter-finals for the first time ever. It was something positive.

'Let's keep this to ourselves, Jeremy. We'll give Johnny J one more day in the sun.'

'Good idea,' I said.

'Good man,' he said. 'Now, those horses aren't going to ride themselves.'

'What horses?' I said.

'Ah sure the cows and hens are only a sideline. It's the horses I make my money on,' he said, and he winked. I hadn't pictured a blind person winking before. 'Get the others, forget the jobs, let's feed them bacon sandwiches and then you're going riding.'

I'd never been riding before. 'OK,' I said.

I ran to the caravan as fast as my legs could carry me. I stopped short of the actual door. It would be hard to face Johnny J for three reasons.

1. The fight the night before.
2. The truth I was keeping from him.
3. I realised I might LIKE Charlie Eastman.

Then I remembered what Jimbo had said. Johnny J deserved one last brilliant day, so I burst through the door and I shook him awake and smiled.

'No matter what, best friends ever,' I said, and he grinned and nodded.

'Best friends ever,' he said. TYSK69

44
The Fall

Walker and Sumo got dressed quickly.

'Just another minute, Charlie,' Sumo called to her as he zipped his fly.

'Take your time,' she said from inside the small room. I explained we were all spending the day riding Jimbo's horses.

Johnny J was really excited. 'I love horses. I mean, I've never actually been on a horse, but I really love them,' he said. Then he furrowed his brow. 'But what about all the jobs?'

'Jimbo wants us to ride horses.'

'Jimbo's the best,' Johnny J said, and he jumped up and down in the caravan, shouting out to the others, 'We're going horse riding!'

Walker shook his inhaler. 'Oh, brilliant! Horses! My favourite!' He was being sarcastic.

'Are they really your favourite?' Sumo said.

'I'll give you one guess.'

'No,' Sumo said, as Walker opened his antihistamine pills and took one. 'I'm too big for horses.'

'Why do you say that?' Charlie asked.

'I'm too big for everything,' he said, and everyone laughed.

After Jimbo and I worked together to feed Charlie and the boys bacon toasties, Jimbo made a call and a man called Brennan arrived up at the house in a tractor and trailer. Jimbo got himself up onto the tractor with ease and told the rest of us to hop on board. Johnny J helped Charlie up and she let him, even though she didn't really need his help. Sumo helped Walker up. I was last in. I was happy to be there with my smiling friends. I didn't dare think about the days that would follow.

Brennan turned to face us. 'Do you like music, kids?'

'Yeah,' Charlie said.

'Good.' He turned on his radio and suddenly we were being blasted with AC/DC's 'That's the Way

I Wanna Rock 'n' Roll'. Sumo headbanged. Walker held his glasses to his sore nose and joined in every now and again until he complained of neck ache.

Jimbo's farm was huge. He may have owned half of Wexford. It just went on and on for what seemed like forever. Then we caught the first glance of the stables, and Betty Bloomers was waiting for us, surrounded by horses. She wasn't in a skirt or bloomers; instead she was wearing a riding hat, jodhpurs and a jacket. She looked cool.

'There you are, kids,' she said. She pointed to the ponies in the enclosure behind her. 'Let's get these beauties tacked up and you riding.'

When Betty took a good look at Walker, she turned to a tall, thin man with a moustache. 'Barry, we're going to need a box for this one.' Then she took a look at Sumo. 'And a bigger ride for this one.'

'No problem, Betty, a box and Freda coming up.'

'Freda? Do you think he'll be all right on Freda?' she said, and Barry looked Sumo up and down and thought about it.

'Ah he'll be fine, won't you, lad?'

'I dunno,' Sumo said.

It turns out that the lonely blind farmer who needed kids to feed his animals and fix his fence wasn't so lonely at all. He had six men working for him and three teenagers who mucked out the stables and a woman named Jessie who ran the office. She popped over just as Barry arrived with Freda.

'So you are the temporary staff Jimbo roped in?'

'Yeah,' I said.

'Well, you gave Barry here a break from milking cows and feeding hens,' Jessie said.

'Much obliged,' Barry said.

'And no one likes fixing that old fence,' Jessie said.

I could see why. I still had blisters.

'So if you kids are ever looking for a job on a farm, you come see me,' she said. Then she took Jimbo by the arm.

'Really?' Sumo said.

'Yeah, really. Enjoy, kids,' he said, and they both walked toward the office beyond the arena.

'Ah brilliant. I'm deffo coming back,' Sumo said, and we were all shocked. I'd never thought of Sumo on a farm. Then again I hadn't really thought of Sumo doing anything other than just being Sumo.

I was given a pony called Juniper. She was chestnut brown and she liked to stamp her feet. It made me nervous, but Betty rubbed her back and she settled.

'She's a pet, our Juniper,' she said. 'Now hop on.'

It was no trouble at all getting on Juniper.

Once I was on, Betty patted my back. 'Well done, Dave,' she said, and she winked at me. She knew I wasn't Dave. She knew everything. That's why she was being so nice.

I looked over at Johnny J. He was on a pony called Bruno. He was petting him and smiling and Barry was showing him how to hang his leg down so he could fix the stirrup so that it was in line with his ankle. He was happy. *Give him one more day*, I heard Jimbo say in my head. *One more day*. My stirrup was already in line with my ankle.

Walker was still trying to hop on his pony called Frank. He was sweating and wheezing already. 'Yeah, I don't know if this is a good idea,' he said, but he kept trying anyway.

'Sit up nice and straight before you put your feet in the stirrups,' Betty said to me, and I straightened up.

'Like this?'

'Exactly like that.'

I shoved my feet in the stirrups and Juniper lifted her front leg and neighed. Betty rubbed her on her side. 'There's a good girl.'

I rubbed her neck. 'Good, Juniper, good,' I said, and Betty grinned and nodded her approval. Juniper dropped her front leg and shook her head. Betty handed me the reins.

'Hold them gently and squeeze with your legs.'

I squeezed really tight.

'Now don't kick too hard, or you might end up the other side of that fence.' Betty pointed to a fence far away in the distance. I stopped squeezing so hard.

Sumo appeared from the stables on Freda. Barry was holding the reins and leading him. Freda was huge. Sumo was still wearing his Wookie mask – we'd all grown used to it and Betty and Barry didn't mention it. He was so excited, and a Wookie on a horse looked so cool.

'I'm on her, lads. I'm on her and she's grand. Look at her!'

Charlie was on a pony called Racer. She was rubbing Racer's ears and whispering sweet things to her. You could already tell Racer and Charlie liked one another. At least that's how it appeared to me.

'Grip with the legs. I don't want to see air between your knee and the saddle.'

I did what I was told.

'And keep your heel down.'

'OK.'

We all started walking. Walker looked really wobbly.

'If you feel wobbly, hold on to Frank's mane.'

Betty mounted her horse Ginger with great ease. Barry mounted one called Loopy and they walked either side of us.

Betty did all the talking. Sumo and Johnny J were bouncing up and down like bouncing balls.

'When walking, sit into the saddle and go with the rhythm. That way you avoid bouncing. You see, like Dave and Brittany here.'

Charlie and I shared a smile. Johnny J worked hard to stop bouncing. Sumo kept on bouncing. Walker lay forward on Frank, holding on to his mane and resting his head on his neck.

'It's really better if you sit up and hold the reins.'

'I'm fine, thanks,' he said, and Betty laughed.

'No trotting for you then?'

'No. I'm fine like this.' He didn't look at all fine.

We walked for a while until Betty felt we were ready to trot.

'Moving to trot, count *one, two* in your head. Up on one, and sit into the saddle for two.' I tried to do what Betty had said, and she nodded. 'Nice. Keep doing exactly that.'

I rubbed Juniper's neck. I was telling her what a good girl she was, when out of nowhere Freda broke into a proper fast gallop. Betty shouted at Sumo to pull the rein left. He tried but he failed. Freda ran like she was looking to gain first place in a race.

Sumo was screaming, 'Oh me, oh my, oh me, oh my . . .'*

Betty set off after him, but Freda was fast. Sumo let go of the reins and hung on to her neck. They were fast approaching the fence. I couldn't hear what Sumo was saying, he was too far ahead, but I guessed it was still, 'Oh me, oh my . . .' and that maybe he was crying. I definitely would have been crying.

---

* 1. Sumo's previous weird sayings included 'Golly gumdrops' and 'Jiminy Cricket'. Anyone else would have been murdered by mean kids.

  2. He also said the phrase 'Please and thank you' when he burped.

  3. Once, his dad farted while putting in a new light bulb in the den. He said, 'I'll take that to go.' Sumo was really like his dad.

Charlie, Walker, Johnny J and I just sat still on our ponies. Barry stayed with us while Betty followed Sumo, then we saw Freda soar over the fence, with Sumo hanging on tight and he fell to the side of her and Charlie gasped, but then he shot back up and clung on to her neck again. Betty and Ginger jumped the fence easily and followed the mad Freda and they all rode off until we couldn't see them any more.

'Don't worry, kids – Betty will sort it,' Barry said, but he looked worried.

'Get me off this thing now,' Walker said, and Barry lifted him down.

We trotted back to the stables, Walker took his pony by the reins and walked beside it. Barry showed us how to brush and feed the ponies. Juniper loved to be brushed and it was fun, but I was concerned that we'd never see Sumo again. I heard him before I saw him.

'Best time ever!' he was shouting.

'Well, it's not something I'd like to see repeated,' Betty said.

'Did you see how fast I went?'

'I saw,' she said. 'I was there.'

We all came out of our stables and there he was

with his mask in his hand and covered head to toe in horse poo.

'I eventually fell off, well, one leg got stuck in a stirrup and Freda dragged me in some poo, but we cleared three fences before that happened!' He was grinning, with horse poo all over his purple face.

'You enjoyed that?' I asked.

'Enjoyed it! I loved it. I'm going to be a jockey when I grow up,' he said, and Betty looked at the size of him and shook her head from side to side.

'Not a jockey, lad, but we'll find something for you.'

'Really? Cos I'm coming back. I swear I am. BEST DAY EVER!'

Johnny J was laughing hard at the poo-covered happy Sumo and so were Walker and Charlie. I smiled, but it was hard to laugh, knowing what lay ahead.

45

The Traitor

Jimbo and Betty brought us to Peter's pub for the Ireland v Romania match at 4 p.m. It was jammed, but Betty and Jimbo got stools and we all sat on the floor in front of the massive screen that was set up on a projector. The pub landlady laid on free sausages and chips and, weirdly, bucketloads of coleslaw!

'Country people love coleslaw,' Sumo said with an air of authority that he didn't usually possess.

Walker nodded his head in agreement. 'Fact,' he said.

Play kicked off and it was really exciting to be sitting in front of a match among a whole village, ooohhing and ahhhing and with some fellas shouting words I'm not even going to mention.

'Come on, lads, get into, will ye?' one man beside us kept saying. There was a woman in the corner praying with rosary beads. During half-time she sprinkled holy water on the projector screen.

'Will you keep the water away from the projector, Bernie? Almighty in heaven, you'll spark the thing out.'

'My dad's right – everyone's mad in their own way,' I said to Charlie, and she laughed.

'It's brilliant though, isn't it, Jeremy?' she said.

'Yeah, it is.'

I had worried that the others wouldn't agree to come to the match, seeing as we'd all talked about keeping a low profile to avoid capture, but Jimbo told me to tell them that no one at the match would be looking at faces in the crowd. All eyes would be glued to the game. He was right. No one noticed us – we just blended right in. It didn't matter though – even as the match started I knew that Jimbo had called the guards and they were on their way. I looked around at my friends and they were happy. I wondered how long it would be before they'd be happy again.

The game finished 0–0, and penalties were needed

to find a winner. Each side scored their opening four, but then Ireland's goalie, Packie Bonner, pulled off what everyone later described as 'a brilliant save' and it was down to a player called David O'Leary to score the penalty and take Ireland into the QUARTER-FINALS OF THE WORLD CUP! Everything and everyone came to a halt in Peter's pub.* The world waited. David O'Leary stood up and blasted the ball into the Romanian net. We'd done it. IRELAND WAS IN THE QUARTER-FINALS OF THE WORLD CUP!

The crowd rose to their feet, with arms in the air, screaming, laughing, hugging, crying, dancing, shouting and singing. What a moment, what a feeling! Sumo and Charlie were right – it was the very best of days. Jimbo shed a tear just, and Betty got up and danced a jig, kicking up her skirts to reveal the big bloomers she loved so much. Johnny J and Charlie danced a jig with her and then she showed them how to square dance. They spun around the room with a lot of others and they were enjoying every second of it and it didn't matter

---

* 1. Time froze. No one ate a sausage, a chip or a spoon of coleslaw.

  2. No one drank a drop or even breathed loud enough to be heard.

  3. Even Bernie stopped praying, and for a moment I forgot I'd betrayed my friends and we were going to kids' jail.

that Johnny J was celebrating with Charlie and I was alone. I wasn't jealous any more.

The pub started to empty out around 9 p.m. Betty drove us all back toward the farm.

'Did you enjoy yourselves, boys?'

'Deadly,' Johnny J said. 'Just deadly.'

We all said it was brilliant and we thanked them for their kindness and then we turned into the farmyard and saw the guards' van with flashing lights in the driveway. I saw the panic in Johnny J's eyes.

'It's going to be OK,' Betty said in a calm voice.

'Oh no. It's too soon,' Johnny J said, and his face paled.

'They know about everything, boy,' Jimbo said. 'It's going to be OK.'

'They can't. It's not time. We need another week. We have to go. Let me out,' he begged.

He panicked and started to try to open his passenger door. I tried to stop him. The locks on the car were manual. There was no central locking that Betty could press to stop a boy who wanted to exit a moving car from doing so. The door swung open and he nearly fell out, but I clung on to him while Betty brought the car to an immediate stop. The two guards came running in our direction. Johnny J struggled from my grip and crawled out onto the gravel driveway.

'She's done for,' he said. 'My mam is done for.' Tears were rolling down his face.

In the car Charlie was crying too. Walker chewed on his lip and Sumo couldn't stand to look at Johnny J, but he took off his Wookie mask and focused on the chickens. I got out of the car and bent down to Johnny J, who was on his knees in tears.

'Just one more week,' he wailed, and he was sobbing so hard it was difficult to hear him.

'I'm so sorry,' I said.

'Jeremy,' Jimbo said, 'it will be fine.' He then spoke to Johnny J. 'Johnny J, your mammy needs you now.'

Johnny J looked up at me with a tear-soaked face. 'You told him?'

'It wasn't like that, boy,' Jimbo said. 'Your faces are everywhere. Betty saw the paper.'

'You knew they were coming for us,' Johnny J said, and he was looking at me as though I was a stranger.

'We have to go home, Johnny J,' I said.

He pushed me away. 'Go away. Go away, Jeremy,' he shouted. He was kneeling on the ground, his head bent low, and everyone standing around him, and he sobbed his heart out. I couldn't watch. My heart felt like a grenade in my chest, rumbling, about to explode. It was the saddest thing I'd ever seen.

A few minutes passed before the two guards helped Johnny J to his feet. We sat in the back of their van in silence. It wasn't a big van, but the others made a point of squeezing together to leave me on my own. Nobody wanted to be near the traitor. Johnny J didn't look around at me once during the long trip home. He just faced the back window and watched the lights on the road. None of the others could look at me either.

The guards sat up at the front of the van. They didn't ask questions. They were waiting till they got us back to Dublin. One of them threw in some bottled water and told us to go to sleep.

'You might as well,' he said. 'It's a long enough trip.'

No one spoke and no one slept the whole way home.

46

The Station

My dad was waiting in the police station. He was sitting next to Uncle Ted and Charlie's mam and to his left sat Sumo's dad and Walker's mam and dad. He'd flown home from Italy. They all stood up when we were marched into the building in a line. One of the guards led the way; me, Johnny J, then Charlie, Walker, Sumo and finally the other guard. There was no escape. They lined us up in front of our parents. I couldn't bring myself to look into my dad's eyes. I didn't know what to say. I could hear Walker sniff and take out his inhaler. His mam started crying.

'And this is why I didn't want you coming down here, Sheila. You're far too emotional,' Mr Brown said.

'Emotional? We're after raising a criminal! How do you want me to be?' she said, and then she started crying again. For the first time in his life Walker didn't know what to do. None of us did, and I think that included our parents. Uncle Ted stepped forward.

'So is it all right if we take the kids home now, guards?' he said. It was after midnight. It had been a very long day and as I looked along the line I realised how messy and tired we all looked. We also smelled.

'Get them to bed and then I want them back here by 9 a.m. tomorrow morning.'

'No problem,' Uncle Ted said.

'Absolutely, guard, thank you,' my dad said.

'You, move it,' Sheila Brown said to Walker. Everyone bar Charlie's mother, Tina Eastman, started to shuffle toward the door.

'Excuse me, guard,' she said, and everyone turned to face her. 'Should we be bringing solicitors along in the morning?'

'That's up to you, love,' the guard said.

'Ah now, come on, they're only kids,' my dad said.

'They broke the law,' one of the guards said.

'Well, how much will a solicitor cost?' Sheila Brown asked in a very shrill voice.

'Oh, they're huge money,' the other guard said. 'I tell you, I wish I'd become a solicitor.'

'My heart bleeds for you,' Mr Brown said to the guard.

'Don't be cheeky to the guard, Denis,' Sheila Brown said to her husband, and Walker laughed.

'Don't you dare laugh,' Denis Brown said to his son. 'I should be in Italy now, and as for the fellas in the job – I'm lucky I wasn't fired!'

'If we can't afford solicitors . . . ?' my dad said, and he gulped the way he always did when he was uncomfortable about something.

'One will be appointed if necessary. In the meantime, you are free to sit with your children while they are being questioned.'

'Ah good, great, that's something,' my dad said. My dad always tries to find the positive in a situation. It's one of the things I really like about him.

'Look, my advice to you is to take those kids home, let them sleep and the questioning can happen in here tomorrow. They have a long day ahead of them,' the guard said, and the parents all nodded.

When we got to the car park, all the other kids said goodbye to one another. No one said goodbye to me. They turned their backs. I understood. I was a traitor after all.

'Johnny J?' I called out as he got into the front passenger seat of his uncle's car. 'I'm sorry,' I said, but he didn't turn around. They just drove away.

I sat in the passenger seat. My dad held on to the steering wheel of the car really tight like he was squeezing it. He didn't turn the car engine on or the lights. He just sat there in the dark squeezing the steering wheel and gritting his teeth for the longest time.

'Are you all right, Dad?' I asked. I thought maybe he was having some kind of medical emergency.

'Am I all right?' he asked. 'Are *you* all right, son?' he said, and he sounded angry.

'Yeah,' I said, but I wasn't.

'Ah good. Well, let me tell you how your mammy is, shall I? She's been crying her eyes out for the past few days. She hasn't eaten. She hasn't slept. She hasn't taken her eye off the phone or the hall door. She's a mess. Your mammy is a mess.'

'Sorry.'

'Sorry? Sorry?! Let me tell you about sorry. Your brother has two black eyes.'

'What? Why?'

'Because he got in a fight with some yoke over you.*

'Oh.'

'Yeah! Oh, and your sister has abandoned nursing school to move back in to mind your mammy, and she's taken King Rupert (my dad called Rachel's boyfriend Rupert 'King Rupert' because he had a posh accent) home with her. His parents are on the phone screaming blue murder because their son should be in medical school, not living in a house of ill repute.'

'What does that mean?'

'It means those poshies think we're a bunch of gangsters, thanks to you.'

'Sorry.'

'Oh, well then, in that case everything is fine, isn't it?' he said, but it was very clear things were not fine. He started the car and we drove home in silence.

Mam was sitting at the bottom of the hall stairs when Dad pushed me through the door. She looked up at me. Her eyes were tired and her hair was a

---

* 1. 'Yoke' was the word my father used for people he didn't like or know.
  2. The yoke was calling us terrible names.
  3. And he was trying to scrape the word 'robber' on the side of Dad's car.

mess. She stood up slowly and uncreased her trousers by patting them down with her two hands.

Dad put his hands up in the air. 'Stay away from him, Debbie. He smells of cow.'

She didn't listen to him. Instead she walked over to me and I immediately felt like I wanted to hug her and run away from her all at the same time. It made me want to cry. She gently tugged my ponytail and looked into my face.

'Are you hurt?'

'No.'

'Has anyone done anything bad to you?'

'No.'

'Have you eaten?'

'Yes.'

'Right, then get up those stairs and get to bed before I kill you,' she said, and she let my hair go and I ran up the stairs as fast as my legs could carry me.

If you'd asked me if I'd be able to sleep after betraying my very best friend and facing criminal charges I would have said, 'NO WAY!' but my eyes were as heavy as my heart and when my head hit my pillow I was gone.

47

The Package

I woke up early the next morning to Rich shaking me furiously.

'Wake up, Numbnutbutt, wake up.'

'I'm awake,' I said, looking at him blearily. His two swollen black eyes were shocking to see.

'Well, well, well, what have you been up to?' he said, and he was grinning as he spoke.

'I messed everything up,' I said, and I started crying again. I couldn't help it. I really wished I could just stop doing that. *What have you got to cry about, Jeremy? Just stop it!*

'What do you mean, you messed everything up?'

Rich said, and he held up two newspapers with the headlines about the Fearless Five. 'You're famous,' he said.

'No, I'm not.'

'You are – there's been loads of reporters here and everything.'

'Yeah?'

'Yeah,' he said, nodding. 'It's been mad. Here, do you think the Fearless Five would be a good name for the band? I'm not sure Fingers & the Fudge is that cool,' he said.

'There's only four of you.'

'Not with Johnny J.'

'He won't be in your band.' *He'll be in England or a prison for kids.*

'Yeah he will, trust me.'

'OK,' I said. I was still half crying and I wasn't in the mood to argue.

'So, the Fearless Five – what do you think?'

'It doesn't work.'

'Maybe. Still, it has a ring to it, doesn't it?'

'Yeah,' I said.

'So what did you do it for?'

'Cos I'm stupid,' I said, and I placed the pillow over my face.

'RICH! Get out of the criminal's room. NOW!' Mam shouted up the stairs.

'Mam called in Father Maloney. You're lucky you're not being exorcised.'

'What's exorcised?' I asked from beneath my pillow.

'It's when they pull demons out of people. I saw it on the TV once, it looks mental, but don't worry, he's only going to do a Mass in the house.'

'Right.'

'Yeah. Mam went totally nuts over this one, Jeremy. Best keep the head down.'

'OK.'

'Rich! Get out of there before I come up these stairs and murder the pair of you.'

'Gotta go,' he said. 'Mam doesn't want you infecting me with your badness.' He chuckled to himself, before rising from my bed and walking to the door. I lifted the pillow.

'Hey, Rich?'

'Yeah?'

'Sorry about your black eyes.'

'Don't be, Esther Banbridge told me I was really

brave.* Before yesterday she didn't know I existed.'

'Nice one,' I said, and I tried to smile but my face wouldn't let me.

Rich gave me the thumbs up and then he left me alone to think about what lay ahead.

When I finally dragged myself out of bed and dared to leave the room, Rachel was waiting and gave me a hug on the landing.

'I don't know what's going on, Jeremy, but I know you and you are good, so let's make an agreement – you give up robbing and I'll give up smoking,' she said, and she smiled and I nodded. 'Deal,' she said.

Rupert came out of Rich's room. He was wearing his hair long like mine, except he didn't have his in a ponytail. It was the first time I thought about cutting my hair.

'Hey ho there, gunslinger,' he said, and Rachel shook her head from side to side.

'Not now, Rupert.'

'I was only saying hello,' he said. He kissed her

---

* 1. Esther Banbridge was the prettiest girl in Rich's class.
  2. She was also the smartest.
  3. She was way out of my brother's league.

forehead. 'I take it now the package is safely returned we can leave?' She smiled at him and nodded. 'Good.' He walked down the stairs.

'What package?' I said.

'You,' he said, and he laughed. 'The Fearless Five – you couldn't make it up.'

I really didn't like Rupert.

48

The Confession

My parents didn't speak to me over breakfast. They were following police orders. I could tell they were dying to know what happened. My mam fidgeted a lot. My dad pretended to read the newspaper. Rich sang to himself.

No one spoke to me and I spoke to no one. Instead I did what Rich told me to do. I kept my head down.

Johnny J and his Uncle Ted were in the police station when my dad and I arrived.

'Hi, Johnny J,' I said, but he ignored me.

Dad pointed to a chair and I sat in it.

'How's Vanessa today, Ted?' he said.

'They're talking about bringing her into the hospital.'

'I'm sorry,' my dad said.

'Thanks,' Uncle Ted said.

I stared at Johnny J. In my head I was pleading with him to look back at me, but he just sat facing the wall.

Walker came in wearing a suit and tie and holding his mother's hand. Charlie soon followed, but this time she was with her father. I'd seen her mam loads of times, going in and out of Johnny J's house, taking care of Johnny J's mam, but I'd never seen her dad close up before. He was a stocky build and he had a massive long red beard. He reminded me of Santa, if Santa wasn't jolly at all.

'Lads,' he said to the men in the room. 'Hello, Sheila.'

'Hello, Declan,' she said.

'So which one of you little toerags is responsible for my daughter robbing a garage and van and running away from home?' he said to us kids.

'Ah now, come on, Declan. I'm sure it's not like that,' Uncle Ted said.

'It certainly is,' Declan Eastman said.

'From what I hear, it's that little girl who caused all of this,' Sheila said.

My head shot up. I was shocked. Why would

Walker tell his mam that Charlie was the cause of all this when it was clearly my fault?!

'Ah now, here,' Declan Eastman said, and he stood up.

Denis Brown stood up as well. He stood, arms folded, while Sheila Brown pointed in Declan Eastman's face.

'She's not as saintly as she looks, so if you want to start pointing a finger, I'd start with pointing fingers at my own if I were you.'

'Don't you dare point at me, Sheila Brown.'

'We weren't supposed to question the kids,' Dad said.

'I'll question my child when and where I want,' Sheila Brown said without even looking at him.

Walker played with his tie and sniffed. He had a big white plaster across his nose and a haunted look in his eye. He was exhausted and probably terrorised. I felt sorry for him. Sheila Brown could frighten a gladiator.

'Now come on, everyone,' Uncle Ted said. 'Just calm down.'

'Can we all be civil now?' my dad said, and I could tell he was uncomfortable.

The kids just sat there, mesmerised and half

terrified by the adults fighting. Sheila and Denis Brown sat back down beside Walker. He kept his head low to avoid glares from Johnny J and Charlie. I was a little relieved I wasn't the only one they were annoyed with. I tried to make eye contact with him but he refused to look my way. I began to wonder what all the others had told their parents. Why Sheila Brown thought Charlie was at fault. *What did Walker say? Why would he blame her? It's all down to me. This was my plan. I did this.*

Sumo and his parents arrived last. I thought maybe if any of my friends would forgive me Sumo would. I looked up at him, but he just shook his head from side to side and sat beside Johnny J. His parents didn't say hello, they didn't nod or wave, instead they just sat down and looked at the floor. It was unsettling to see Mary and Gerry Lane so low. Normally they were so friendly and chatty. I realised we probably wouldn't be welcome in their son's den any more. *Gutted.* Then again, even if the others were, I wouldn't be. Nobody liked me now. *Really gutted.* Of course, that probably didn't matter anyway, because I'd be locked up in a cell with Stab-a-Rasher. *Really, really gutted.*

Everyone waited in the silence for a guard to come and tell us what was to happen next. My stomach twirled and swirled and I wondered whether or not I'd be sick. *Can I be charged with vomiting in a police station? Is it illegal to vomit in a police station? Can they put me in a cell? If they do, I hope they give me a bucket.*

When Johnny J's Auntie Alison swanned in, she wasn't alone; she had a man with her. He wore an expensive suit and round spectacles and he carried a briefcase. I guessed he was a solicitor. He immediately went to the duty officer's window. No one was there. He rang the bell.

Johnny J's Auntie Alison stood in the middle of the room looking around at everyone and it was clear she wasn't impressed by what she saw. We all just stared at her like she was some kind of exotic animal until Uncle Ted stood up.

'What are you doing here, Alison?'

'My nephew's in trouble, Ted.'

'Who's with Vanessa?'

'I've hired a nurse.'

'You shouldn't be here,' he said, and he looked upset.

She ignored him. 'Well, isn't this just perfect?'

she said to everyone and no one. 'It's not like we don't have enough problems.'

'Auntie Alison . . .' Johnny J said, but she put her hand up to stop him from speaking.

'You've done enough, thank you, Johnny.'*

'Leave the boy alone,' Uncle Ted said.

'Why not let him get away with robbery while his mother –' She stopped herself, pursed her lips, took a deep breath and calmed herself. 'He needs structure,' she said. 'Stability. Someone to teach him right from wrong.'

'Don't you dare . . .' Ted said, and he looked really angry.

'He's coming with me, Ted,' she said, and I looked over at Johnny J and his eyes were bulging to the point of bursting. He was genuinely scared. I was scared too. My stomach twisted into a knot. *I might need that bucket.* Charlie's hand started to shake. I wanted to say something to her to make her feel OK, but I couldn't. It wasn't OK and she hated me.

'You need to stop talking now,' Uncle Ted warned

---

* 1. Auntie Alison always called Johnny J 'Johnny'.
  2. He hated when she did that.
  3. And right then and there I hated her.

Auntie Alison in a quiet but firm voice, and she stopped talking. Ted sat down.

'Ted?' Johnny J said, and his voice sounded weird, like it was broken.

'It's OK, Johnny J. You're going nowhere.'

'Except maybe to prison,' Auntie Alison said, under her breath, but everybody heard.

'Ah now, hold on, there's no need for that,' my dad said.

'There's every need,' she said. 'They're a bad influence.' She pointed to Uncle Ted. 'In fact, you're a bad influence.' I thought that was harsh. Uncle Ted hadn't robbed any garages (that I knew of). Uncle Ted hung his head, but my dad stood up.

'Ted Tulsi has been a father figure to that boy all his life. He's one of the best men I know,' he said. 'I will not hear one word against him.'

Mr Brown stood up and so did Mr Lane. Mr Eastman stood up and even Sheila Brown. Every adult in the room was on their feet and standing beside Uncle Ted, facing Auntie Alison down.

I have no idea what they were planning next, but I was in a panic, so I stood up and I blurted out, 'It wasn't Johnny J. It wasn't Uncle Ted or Charlie or Walker or Sumo. It was me! I made them do it!' The whole room turned to stare at me and I thought I might faint. Just then two detectives walked out of a side door.

'Fair enough, sunshine, we'll start with you then.'

Ah nuts!

49

The Interview

My dad and I both swallowed hard and followed the detectives into a small grey room. We sat down opposite them.

'He didn't mean that,' Dad said.

'Did you?' the older one with ear hair said.

'It was me,' I said, mesmerised by his ear hair.*

'Stop saying that,' Dad said.

'Why don't we take it from the start?' the younger fella with fangs said.

So I told them the story of the Fearless Five. I talked about Johnny J's mam and how sick she

---

* 1. He was the older of the two men.
  2. He wore a suit but it was worn and he smelled of really strong aftershave.
  3. His ear hair was bright orange.

was. I told them how the Irish medical system was failing her but the American one was brilliant.

Detective Earhair looked at his notes. 'Yes, a Mrs Shanley mentioned America in her statement.'

'Who is Mrs Shanley?' my dad asked.

'Tulsi's neighbour, old dear . . .' Detective Earhair said.

'Owner of approximately fifteen cats,' Detective Fangs said.*

'We just wanted to save her, and they can do that in America,' I said, and my dad sighed deeply and grabbed my hand in his.

'Who told you that?' Detective Earhair asked.

'Walker?'

'Is that the little fella?' he asked, looking at his notes.

'He's very smart,' I said. I explained how he'd won the Young Scientist award for his older sister, but they weren't interested in that.

'Let's stick to the robberies,' Detective Earhair said.

---

* 1. Every now and then he'd lick the underside of one of his fang teeth.
  2. He was wearing a leather jacket over a crisp white shirt, and a big fat red tie hung from his neck.
  3. He looked like a cartoon character, except he wasn't funny or cool or even very frightening.

I talked them through the two robberies, the letter, the ticket, the escape and our time in Wexford. When I finished, my dad was flabbergasted.

'You did all that for Mrs Tulsi?' my dad asked.

'And Johnny J,' I said.

'Ah, son,' he said. 'Ah now, isn't that something?' he said to the two men in front of him. He looked as if he wanted to cry or something. He squeezed my hand. He didn't seem angry any more.

'Yeah, it is,' Detective Fangs said. 'It's robbery, aggravated assault and battery.'

'Ah fair cop to the robbery, but who was assaulted and battered?' my dad said.

'They tied up a security guard, held him down and threatened him with pepper spray,' Detective Fangs said.

'Where did you get the pepper spray?' Detective Earhair asked, and I looked at my dad and he went purple.

'My wife got it in America,' Dad said.

'Do you know that's illegal in Ireland, Mr Finn?' Detective Fangs said to my dad.

'Eh, no. We had no idea,' my dad said. He's a very bad liar.

'Sorry, Dad.'

'That's OK, son.'

'The assault and battery charges are also for locking Mrs Roland into the toilets.'

'That's hardly assault and battery!' my dad said.

'It's OK, Dad,' I said. 'I'll do my time.'

'You will not. It'll be all right, son. Your dad's sorting this one.' He winked at me and I was so relieved.

'Thanks, Dad,' I said, and a tear slid down my face. I swore I would stop crying after that day. If I escaped detention I'd be going into secondary school in September! *Come on, Jeremy. Crying has to stop!*

'Where is this letter you say that Johnny J sent?' Detective Earhair said.

'I dunno. We posted it days ago.'

'Get on that?' he said to Detective Fangs, who nodded and took a note of it.

'Jeremy, do you realise how serious this all is?' Detective Earhair said.

'I do,' I said, and I was crying again.

'Have you ever stolen before?' he asked.

'NEVER!'

'Are you planning on stealing again?'

'NEVER, EVER!' I said.

Detective Earhair nodded to himself and took some notes. 'This is very serious,' he said, and he shook his head sadly.

I felt my stomach lurch, then my insides heat up and it came like a wave. I put my hands to my mouth and tried to hold it in, but the vomit slipped through my fingers and gushed onto the desk. Detective Fangs was up and out of his seat in a second. Detective Earhair didn't move. He just sighed and looked at my horrified father.

'Well, the good news is that this fella won't make any kind of criminal. He doesn't have the stomach for it.'

My dad nodded and grabbed a hankie from his pocket and wiped vomit from his shoes.

50

The Caution

They took everyone's statement that day.

Uncle Ted found the letter with the money and instructions to use the ticket and to get an American visa. The envelope had been in a huge pile of unopened post. Johnny J's mam had been too sick for anyone in the Tulsi household to worry about opening letters, so it was just sitting there in a stack of paper, resting on the cushion of the bench beside the hall door. We could have stayed away the full two weeks and that letter would still probably never have been opened. We hadn't thought about that! The guards took the letter as evidence for the DPP.*

---

* 1. The DPP stands for the Director of Public Prosecutions.
  2. They decide if they are going to charge people who commit crimes.
  3. They sent Freaky Fitzer's older brother Tomo to kids' prison for shoplifting. (A LOT of shoplifting.) We were armed robbers!

Later that evening we were cautioned (which means the police let us know in writing we'd done a very bad thing), but the good news was they were much nicer to us when they realised why we'd done the robberies. Detective Earhair described our reasons as altruistic, which means unselfish. My dad said altruistic described us perfectly. He said we should be known as the Altruistic Five.

Sheila Brown wasn't impressed. She didn't care why we'd done it. She said it was stupid. It was a criminal act and it threatened her son's future. She didn't want Walker hanging around with us any more. She was glad he was going to a posh school for genius kids.

Everyone else's parents were really relieved. They chatted to one another.

'Good intentions,' Mrs Lane said with a sigh.

'Ah, great intentions,' Mr Eastman said.

'God love them, the very best of intentions,' my dad said.

Uncle Ted couldn't talk. He was too emotional. He was red-faced and biting his lip hard, but he held on to Johnny J and ruffled his hair a lot.

Mr Brown was nodding along with everyone until Mrs Brown gave him a belt. 'Good intentions, my eye,' Mrs Brown said. Then she turned to Walker. 'How can an intelligent boy like you be so stupid?'

'Bad influence,' Auntie Alison said, and then she and her solicitor were escorted into the back room to talk business with the police, leaving our proud and relieved parents a little stunned.

'That's a cold woman,' my dad said, and Uncle Ted nodded.

'She wasn't always like that,' he mumbled. Then he ruffled Johnny J's hair again and hugged him tight against his chest. 'Let's go home, Johnny J. Your mammy is waiting.'

Before they could move, Auntie Alison's solicitor appeared in the doorway. 'Johnny, could we see you in here for a minute or two?' Johnny J looked to Uncle Ted for guidance. 'It will only take a short time, I promise,' the man said. He smiled at Uncle Ted. 'I'll take care of him.'

Uncle Ted nodded. 'I'll wait in the car,' he said.

Mrs Lane gave me a hug in the car park and told me I'd be welcome in their den anytime. Sumo wasn't talking to me though, so she was probably wrong about that.

I got into the front passenger seat of the car. Johnny J was still inside the police station with his

Auntie Alison. I wondered what was happening to him. My dad had forgotten his jacket in the station so he left me waiting in the car. Uncle Ted saw me alone and came and sat in behind the wheel of my dad's car.

'Hiya, Jeremy,' he said.

'Hiya, Uncle Ted.'

He grinned at me. 'So it was your plan?'

'Sorry.'

'Nah, don't be. You didn't want to give up on Johnny J's mammy. You thought you could do something to save her. What you all did was very wrong, but I want you to know that I think you've a big heart and I'm proud to know you.'

He put out his hand to shake mine. I shook it. He was smiling at me but he looked very sad.

'Do you think Johnny J will ever forgive me?' I asked Uncle Ted.

'For what?'

'Jimbo said I needed to bring Johnny J home.'

'Jimbo was right.'

'Johnny J thinks I gave us up.'

'Johnny J is going through a very hard time and he's angry and scared, that's all.'

'So he'll forgive me?'

'He will.'

'OK.'

Ted stood out of the car.

'Uncle Ted?'

'Yeah?'

'Will Johnny J's mam die soon?' I asked.

'Yeah, son, she will,' he said, and his voice trembled a little and he blinked hard.

'I'm really sorry.'

'Me too,' he said, and he gave me a sad smile.

'Will Auntie Alison take Johnny J away from us?'

'Not as long as there is breath in my body,' Uncle Ted said.

'Really?' I said, and my heart soared a little in my chest.

'I'm going to fight for him,' Uncle Ted said. 'After all, I have been like a dad to him all his life.'

'That's right,' I said.

'Let's keep that to ourselves for now,' he said.

'OK. I swear. I won't say a word. You can trust me. I'm really not a traitor,' I said.

'I know that, Jeremy.'

And for the first time I knew that even though everything was terrible and sad and messy, things would eventually be good again.

51
The Future

When the press discovered why we'd done what we'd done, the story just grew and grew, and within two days the Fearless Five were nearly as big as the Irish team. (Well, in one small suburb of Dublin anyway.) Reporters were knocking on our doors and photographers were sent to take our photos. In the end they took photos of our whole families and we all wore our Sunday best and everyone wanted to know how poor Vanessa Tulsi was and strangers all over the country said that they were praying for her. We got cards sent to us – most were really nice but a few mentioned we were going to hell. People we didn't even know smiled and waved at us and gave us the thumbs up. I figured at the time that the DPP must have taken public opinion, because they closed the case very quickly and we were free!*

Sheila Brown decided we weren't so bad after all when she realised that being associated with the Fearless Five was a positive thing for Walker. That was good news. It meant that Walker could hang around with us for one last summer, even if he'd forget about us when he went to his posh school.

On the day that the Irish team met the Pope my mam insisted on bringing me with her to visit Johnny J's mam in the hospital.

'But Johnny J's not talking to me, Mam.'

'Of course he is. Don't be an eejit.' My mam wasn't as proud of my plan as my dad or Uncle Ted. 'Robbery is robbery, assault is assault and battery is battery,' she'd said after the photographer had finished taking our family photo for the paper. 'Don't think that you're some hero. Good intentions

---

* 1. Rolands' and the security company both declined to press charges.
  2. The travel agent refunded the ticket.
  3. Uncle Ted gave back the spending money we'd put in the envelope for Johnny J's mam, and our parents paid back the money we'd spent on train tickets, ice cream, chips and burgers.

351

or bad intentions, it doesn't matter – a criminal is a criminal.'

I really didn't want to go to see Johnny J's mam. The idea scared me, but Mam gave me no choice so I went, and I'm really glad I did.

Uncle Ted was waiting in the hospital corridor.

'How is she, Uncle Ted?'

'Having a good day,' he said, and my mam instantly cheered up. Johnny J was in the room with his mother.

'Vanessa would love to see you, Jeremy,' Uncle Ted said.

'Why?' I said.

'Don't be rude,' my mam said.

'She wants to thank you.'

'Ah no, it's OK. I'll wait here.' I was terrified. The last time I'd seen her she looked so sick. This time she would look paler, sicker, her veins might even be fatter, bigger. I just couldn't bear it. I didn't want to see her.

'Ah no. Tell her I said she's welcome.' But Mam pushed me through into the room and suddenly there I was, standing in front of Mrs Tulsi and Johnny J. Mrs Tulsi was sitting propped up on a lot of pillows. She had a needle in her hand with a tube coming out of it and it was hooked up to a plastic bag of liquid hanging above her head. That made my stomach turn so I looked away. Johnny J was sitting in the chair beside her. He cast his eyes to the floor as soon as I walked in, but she smiled at me, a big warm smile, like she used to before she was sick. When she was smiling, she really didn't look that bad at all.

'There he is,' she said.

'Hiya, Mrs Tulsi.'

'Hiya, Jeremy.' She patted the bed. 'Why don't you sit here?'

I wanted to run but I didn't. I just perched on the smallest corner of the bed. It was really uncomfortable.

'I have a lot to thank you for,' she said.

'Robbing is bad,' I said. I don't know why I said it. I was nervous and I could hear my mam in my head, saying, 'Don't forget you're not a hero – a criminal is what a criminal does.'

'Robbing is bad,' she agreed, 'but bringing my son home to me is good.'

Johnny J looked up and his eyes blazed. He was still angry.

'It was brave to risk losing your best friend to

353

do the right thing, and even if it felt wrong, it was the right thing. I think that you are the best friend my son will ever have.'

I wanted to cry. *Stop crying! Please stop crying!* Johnny J looked away.

'Now make up, the both of you,' she said, 'and stop all this messing.'

'Yes, Mrs Tulsi,' I said.

She looked at Johnny J. 'Well?'

'OK, Mam,' he said.

She took a fiver out from under her pillow. 'Go buy yourselves some ice creams, and send your mammy in to me, won't you, Jeremy.'

'Yes, Mrs Tulsi.'

Johnny J bought us choc ices in the hospital shop and we walked outside onto the grass and sat under a tree. We didn't talk about Johnny J's mam or the press attention we received, even though that was really cool. We didn't talk about the fight and he didn't look so angry any more. We just talked.

'Did you hear Father Maloney is making us do penance?' I said.

'What kind of penance?' Johnny J said.

'We have to do jobs for him or something,' I said.

'What?'

'Yeah, Mam and Sheila Brown organised it for all of us. Mam said it will teach us that good people do good things. Sheila Brown says it will look good for the papers.'

'All of us.'

'Yeah.'

'I might not be here. Auntie Alison is determined to take me to England.'

'That's not happening,' I said.

He shook his head from side to side and he battled to suck back a bulging tear. I looked away.

'This is your home,' I said, looking up into the big blue sky. 'It's where you belong, with Sumo, Walker, me and . . .'

'. . . Charlie?' he said, and I nodded.

'And Charlie,' I said, and he smiled.

'Anyway, what kind of jobs?' he asked.

'I dunno – cleaning the church, helping auld ones and the choir.'

'Oh no.'

'I know.'

'This is going to be really terrible,' he said.

'Yeah,' I agreed. 'Are you joining Rich's band?'

'Would you mind if I did?'

'No, I'd like it,' I said, and I was telling the truth. I saw how happy Johnny J was on the stage. I wanted him to be happy.

'Really?'

'Yeah. I was thinking of managing it,' I said.

'No way?' He sounded happy about that.

'I think I'd be a good manager,' I said.

'You'd be deadly,' he said.

'Cool.'

'Maybe things won't be so bad after all,' he said, but then his eyes darkened and I knew he was thinking about his mam.

'Ireland made it into the quarter-finals of the World Cup, so anything can happen. Right?'

'That's true,' he said. 'Father Maloney described it as a miracle when he was visiting my mam.'

'There you go,' I said, and he smiled. Miracles happen. 'No matter what, everything is going to be OK.'

We were facing one last summer together before everything would possibly change. I promised myself to relax and not to worry so much. Of course there were still things to worry about, mainly the Auntie Alison problem. Uncle Ted had a battle on his hands.

Father Maloney was making us do acts of penance. *Slightly worrying.* Rich was being really nice to me. *Definitely worrying.* We were known as the Fearless Five now, and everywhere we went people knew us. That could cause problems. *How can we have fun if everyone is watching?* I'd just promised my very best friend that, no matter what, everything was going to be OK. I needed a new plan.

A day later Ireland lost to Italy in the quarter-finals and the dream of Ireland winning the World Cup died, but the country still celebrated. The boys in green came home to a heroes' welcome, and it didn't matter that they lost, it only mattered that they'd tried. When my mam told me that I had to spend a whole day scraping wax from the floor of the Holy Mary Mother of Sorrows Church, I told her that maybe it didn't matter that my friends and I did something bad, it only mattered that we'd tried to do something good. She thought about it for less than a second. 'No! It matters. Now get scraping.'

And so our time as wanted criminals came to an end, but we still had a whole summer ahead to laugh, cry, win, lose and love. You see, even if we couldn't save Johnny J's mam, maybe we could still save Johnny J and Uncle Ted from Auntie Alison and England. Our summer was just getting started. We had a band to break out, a family to save and a really annoying priest to shake off, and I had a new plan. But that's a whole other story . . .

About the Author

Bannie McPartlin lives in an ancient city once inhabited by Vikings and now Dublin people. She's married to Donal, a drummer, guitar and piano player. He's a man of many noises. Together they have four dogs: Trudy, Bonzo, Misty and Doris. Bannie has written fiction for adults for over ten years under the name Anna, but the kids she loves in her life call her Bannie, so the name change is for them.